Nancy Amelia Wakefield

Over the River and Other Poems

Nancy Amelia Wakefield

Over the River and Other Poems

ISBN/EAN: 9783744711760

Printed in Europe, USA, Canada, Australia, Japan

Cover: Foto ©Andreas Hilbeck / pixelio.de

More available books at **www.hansebooks.com**

AND

OTHER POEMS

BY

MRS. N. A. W. (PRIEST) WAKEFIELD

BOSTON
LEE AND SHEPARD, PUBLISHERS
NEW YORK
CHARLES T. DILLINGHAM
1883

PREFATORY NOTE.

THE reader will kindly allow a few moments by way of introduction to this volume of poems. It comes not demanding attention and challenging fame, but shrinkingly yielding to the solicitation of friends. Mrs. S. B. Priest, the mother of the author, has cherished the purpose of giving her daughter's writings to the press for several years, as she has always felt a warrantable pride in these productions. This purpose has been stimulated by the frequent request of relatives and other friends, far and near, that they might have an opportunity of owning a collection of the poetical works of " Nancy Priest " in the form of a printed volume. So large a number have signified their intention to take one or more copies, that the mother feels warranted in making this venture, hoping that the expense of publishing may at least be reimbursed by the sale of the volume. The writer of this note, by earnest request, has been induced to undertake the task of arranging the papers, and preparing a brief memoir of the author, though sincerely desiring that the work might be placed in more competent hands.

If the fame of Mrs. Wakefield had been the chief object in this publication, the number of the pieces would have been **considerably less.** Only a few of these fugitive verses will become classics and survive the fashion of the year, though very few have been admitted which are unworthy of reprint. But it is true that the collections of our popular poets contain many titles which are short-lived, though pretty, elegant and interesting. However, being composed for an occasion, or springing from the pressure of current events, they are not made for all time, or even for the next generation. But there are some specimens of poetry in this collection which bear the stamp of genius, and have already found their appropriate place in the great repositories of selected poetical inspiration.

The best known of this class is entitled "Over the River," and has been read with tearful eyes and admiring taste by uncounted thousands in our own and other lands. It is many years since the words had been set to music by six or eight different composers. From the nature of its subject, it appeals to the universal heart of mankind, while its form and language are the perfect vehicle of the sentiment. One cannot conceive that any thing can make it less popular a hundred years hence

than it is to-day. Though it cannot compare with
Gray's " Elegy " in finished elegance of expression, yet
it has a music, a rhythm, a pathos which is unsurpassed.
Its consoling power has been tested in the experience of
a great multitude of bereaved families, and its healing
power is not lessened by time. Surely one has not lived
in vain to whom it has been given to speak words of
solace, comfort and hope to millions of aching hearts, in
measures which cling to the memory and infuse the soul
with a heavenly calm.

There are other poems in this volume which evince
equal genius, though, perhaps, no other has such elements
of enduring popularity. The one entitled " Heaven "
has been much admired, and has found its place in one
or more collections of the choicest poetry in the English
language. Without specifying, it may be said that there
are between ten and twenty poems in this book which
cannot be read without deep emotion.

But, as the design of this publication was to please
friends, many pieces have been inserted, whose interest
and value are chiefly personal or local, or both combined.
The local and personal associations will pass away, when
the poems will cease to have many readers ; yet these
poems have great merit, nevertheless. They have pleased
and cheered and charmed those who were dear to the
author, and so have proved their worth. They are re-

plete with sense and **sensibility**. There is not **a silly or** soft line in **them** all ; they are the **outpourings of a** strong mind and **passionate** heart, all under the control of high **moral and** religious principle.

It was **a** question **whether** the poems should be arranged in any particular order, **or** thrown into a mass without any **plan** of combination. **If the** date of each could have been determined, probably they **would have** been placed in chronological order, and thus left to exhibit the growth **and** the tone **of the writer's mind in** successive years. But this was impossible. **It was then** concluded to make an effort at assortment, and arrange the poems under several heads. The result is shown in the following **pages.** It was soon found to be impossible to make a perfect classification, as several pieces under **the** divisions of " Religious," **" Love and** Friendship," " Elegiac Poems," and perhaps some others, are interchangeable. **Still,** it is believed that the greater number are in their appropriate sections.

One trait of Mrs. Wakefield's **mind will** attract the attention of every intelligent reader. It was her power of entering into the spirit **and** the surroundings of her imaginary characters. This **is** evinced in numerous cases ; but the power of putting herself in another's place **is seen in " The Hour before Execution," in "** The Magdalen," in " The Midnight Bivouac," **and** many others, with special distinctness. The greater part of the " Patriotic " pieces show how Mrs. Wakefield entered into the very life and spirit of the soldiers, and how deeply she sympathized with the anxious ones at home. The poem entitled " War to the Knife, and the Knife to the Hilt " cannot be read without a shudder. It is an heroic and awful strain, as terrible as the fiercest lines in the " Marseillaise Hymn." The reader must remember that it was written in the darkest hours of the war, when the very life of the nation was in peril. The writer felt no personal animosity ; but she loved her country and longed to see its assassins smitten. Her heart was one of peculiar tenderness, and she would have ministered to a wounded foe with gentle helpfulness. The songs of patriotism are alone sufficient to recommend the whole volume to those who fought our country's battles, and all those who rejoiced in the triumph of freedom.

The " Miscellaneous Poems " which fill the closing pages are of varied merit, and, except a few amusing trifles, are worthy of a place. See, for example, " Katie blowing Bubbles," " Bertha's Christmas," and others. With these explanations and remarks, the volume is left to its fortunes, with the assured belief that many will give it a warm reception, and cherish it as a peculiar treasure.

A. P. M.

LANCASTER, MASS., September, 1882.

CONTENTS.

MEMOIR.

THE events in the life of Mrs. Wakefield may be related in a few words. She was born on the seventh day of December, 1836. Her full maiden name was Nancy Amelia Woodbury Priest. Her father, Francis Dana Priest, was a native of Gardner, Mass., and of respectable parentage. The mother of Mr. Priest was the daughter of Col. Jacob Woodbury, a leading man in Winchendon, Mass., and famous in his day as a Revolutionary veteran, and for his exploit in pursuing and slaying a wolf. Mrs. Sophia B. Priest, the mother of Nancy, is a member of the Hale family, numerous and respected in every generation since the settlement of the town.

Though the home of the family was in Winchendon during nearly the whole of their early and their married life, yet it so happened that Mr. and Mrs. Priest, who were united in marriage in February, 1835, moved into the easterly edge of Royalston a few months before the birth of their gifted child. Thus Winchendon lost the honor of being the birthplace of Nancy Priest. After two or three years, the family returned to Winchendon, where they have continued to reside, with the exception of three or four years in Hinsdale, N.H., between 1851 and 1855.

Nancy never attended school after leaving Winchendon, when in her fifteenth year, except for a term or two in Bernardston in 1858. "She was never from home," says her mother, "any length of time till married, which took place December 22, 1865." Her husband, Lieut. Arrington Clay Wakefield, had made an honorable record in the war of the Rebellion, then brought to a triumphant close by the success of the national arms. They had three children. The eldest, Francis Arrington (born July 6, 1867), and their second, Harry Cavino (born May 28, 1869), are still living (1882) with their father. Their only daughter, Alice Emma (born on the 27th of August, 1870), died on the 15th of the following September. Six days later Mrs. Wakefield followed her child into the fold of the Good Shepherd.

Such are the outline facts in the life of one who lived about thirty-four years in the privacy of home, and never attracted notice except by the publication of an occasional poem. And, as these were generally anonymous, the author was heard of by few outside of her immediate neighborhood until after her lamented decease. " Lizzie

Lincoln," an alliterative *pseudonyme*, after the fashion of the time, became familiar to a portion of the reading public, while the name of the real author was unknown. Yet that quiet life was full of an inner history, — the history of a mind, heart, and soul, which labored with a peculiar intensity, as is proved by nearly every thing which found expression in verse. The life of the author, in this case, is to be read in her writings. Judged by these, she had a strong, clear mind, a heart full of the deepest and sweetest sensibilities, and a moral and spiritual nature of the purest and most elevated type.

Without being a precocious child, she evinced superiority to the ordinary run of children in many ways which mothers and other members of a family are apt to observe. "She learned all the letters of the alphabet, great and small," writes her mother, "in the summer before she was two years old." As she was born in December, we are left to infer that she had learned the alphabet when not much over a year and a half in age. At this early date she would "tell her age, and repeat short verses." It is reported of her, when about two years old, that "nothing ever pleased her like hearing reading and singing." No instance is remembered when she ever tore a *good-looking book*, articles which most children treat with little regard. While still in childhood she "used to write poetry on her slate, and rub it out quickly if it was likely to be read." This shyness about exposing her lines to the eyes of others, characterized her through life. Her facility in making rhymes was soon found out by her schoolmates, who used to coax her to make poetry for them. And in this way much was extorted from her in after years, for particular occasions, and sometimes for the press.

Something of her peculiarities may be learned from the following extract of a letter written by a respected Baptist minister, the pastor of her parents, the Rev. Andrew Dunn : —

"She showed in early life a strong desire for books, and made them her companions by giving herself to reading and meditation. A slight acquaintance with her in her childhood, would fail to impress any one with the idea that she possessed peculiar traits of mind, which betokened future greatness, as she was retiring in her habits, and very reserved in the presence of strangers; being rather indifferent to the common affairs of every-day life, willing that other members of the family should work or play, if she could be left undisturbed in her reading and meditations. Her love of books conduced to make her in school one of the best scholars of her age. Her readiness to acquire knowledge, and to comprehend the reason of things, while quite young, showed the careful observer that she possessed powers of mind above mediocrity. She seemed to know, as by intuition or abstract thought, what others acquired by hard study."

The independent working of her mind was observable in her childhood. Mr. Dunn, who knew her in school, as well as in the family and the church, continues, —

"She was truly self-made according to her own ideal type, as she would make no one her model of imitation. It was early manifest that the Muses charmed her; for, as she mused, the fire burned in her mind to express her thoughts in verse. Those who peruse the productions of her pen, and consider the disadvantages under which she labored, will be convinced that she was a natural poet; and, had her life been continued a few years longer, her poetical works would have been greatly augmented and enriched."

She enjoyed the usual advantages of common-school education in a town where the schools held a high rank in comparison with those of other places. During the latter part of the time, she attended the academy, then taught by the Rev. Mr. Wilmarth, and made good improvement of her time as a diligent and conscientious girl. In 1851, when she was about fifteen, the family, as said above, removed to Hinsdale, N.H., from which time she ceased to attend school, except for a short period at Bernardston, under Professor Ward of Powers Institute. In the following collection of poems, two will be found relating to her removal from Winchendon to Hinsdale. One of them purports to have been written at the age of fourteen. These little poems have no special merit, but are inserted as a part of her autobiography, and as evincing her varying moods of mind in view of moving away from the scenes and the friends of her childhood.

The poem entitled " Over the River," which has carried the author's name wherever the English language is read, was written while the family was living in Hinsdale, and probably not long before their return to Winchendon. This would fix it at about her twentieth year. At the time she was living at home and working in a paper-mill. One day at the noon closing, while the hands were gone to dinner, she remained, as usual, because the family resided at some distance. As she sat on a sack of rags, looking across the Ashuelot which flows through the village, the impulse in her breast moved her to write. The origin of the poem is given in an article prepared for a magazine by the Rev. E. S. Best, a Methodist clergyman, who once had an appointment in Winchendon. According to him, the poem was put to paper in a stormy day, while the author was gazing through the dusty window-panes. " Over the misty current her dark eyes gleam with a mysterious brilliancy. She picks up a piece of paper, and with her pencil writes rapidly for a few minutes : but the bell rings ; the machinery begins to clatter ; she thrusts the paper into her pocket, and resumes her work. On that crumpled paper is written the first sketch of a poem which has gained a well-de erved renown." The author of the poem, in a letter to the brother of a musical composer who desired to set it to music, gave the following account of its origin : —

"The little poem to which he purposes to give musical expression was written originally on a sheet of brown wrapping-paper, in the 'hour's nooning' at the mill, and then carried home, thrown in with other loose papers, and entirely forgotten until I came across it by accident again, while looking for something else, more than a year after."

It is stated in addition, by her mother, that the manuscript came near being destroyed soon after it was written, but was happily rescued from an inglorious fate. It was left in a dress which was about to be washed, when Mrs. Priest, in emptying the pocket, found the bit of crumpled brown paper, and so saved the priceless poem which the author so strangely forgot.

It has been suggested, that she may have written other poems equal or superior to the one which made her name famous, because she destroyed very many which were never seen by any eyes but her own. "Several times she has gone to her desk, gathered up all her papers, and cast them into the fire." She did not seem to appreciate her own writings, and could not be convinced that they had any special merit. The fact that she forgot all about "Over the River" makes it credible that other flashes of inspiration passed through water or fire.

But whatever Miss Priest wrote was her own. She

never consciously plagiarized a line, or borrowed an idea or an image. Her measure, also, was the vibration of her own exquisitely strung organization. A controversy which arose in regard to the originality of "Over the River" gave her great pain. The poem first appeared in "The Springfield Republican," August 22, 1857, when she was in her twenty-second year. The editor was informed that the reputed author, "Lizzie Lincoln," had imposed upon him by sending him the production of another writer. When the question was put to her as to the originality of the poem, her reply was that she could not tell: "she only knew that she had written it." When the imputation of untruthfulness and of literary piracy first came to her knowledge, she burst into tears, and "expressed regret that she had ever written a stanza." The editor of the Western paper who had started the accusation was obliged, on examination, to confess his mistake. The reputation of the author was vindicated; but a wound had been inflicted which was never entirely healed. She could not be persuaded to enter upon a course of authorship, or even, except by strong persuasion, to write occasional pieces for the press.

The writer of these pages recalls a fact which fairly exhibits the extreme modesty of Miss Priest. In making preparation for the centennial celebration of the incorporation of the town of Winchendon in November,

1864, by which time our poetess had become widely and favorably known to the public, she was requested to write a hymn to be sung on the occasion. It is republished here in the "Miscellaneous" division. As she felt a deep interest in the event, the request was readily complied with; and the citizens were more than satisfied with the production. When I took the poem, after looking it over, I gave her two dollars as compensation, but with a sense of mortification that I was not able to give a larger sum. But she was surprised at the liberality of the offer, and, with difficulty, was induced to accept the money. She blushed like a child at the thought that her trifle was so highly appreciated. The occurrence, which I have often recalled with amused interest, was recently confirmed by her mother, after eighteen years have intervened, by informing me how surprised Nancy was at receiving such compensation for what she had scribbled off at a sitting.

A writer in "The Springfield Republican," soon after the decease of Mrs. Wakefield, recalled a scene in the girlhood of one whom so many had learned to love, through her writtings, who had never seen her face. He says, —

"I was more than sorry to hear that the gifted author of 'Over the River' had passed

'From sight with the boatman pale
To the better shore of the spirit land.'

I knew her when, in 1858, she was a pupil of Professor Ward, at Powers Institute, Bernardston, Mass. She was rather a shy, quiet girl, very much absorbed in her studies, but always pleasant and obliging. My most prominent recollection of her is of a grave little figure bending persistently over a book, with a profusion of black curls falling around, and almost hiding, her intellectual face. I had always the impression that she had a different motive for study from many of her younger and gayer companions; that she either loved knowledge for its own sake, or had reached that age of experience where she realized the true value of education and culture. I think few of the scholars knew of her literary reputation. The first intimation I had of it was at the close of the fall term. Hon. H. W. Cushman, at one time lieutenant-governor of Massachusetts, had offered the young ladies connected with the school a prize for the best original essay, and she was one of the competitors. Rev. Mr. Ranney, in his speech before awarding the prizes, said it was honor enough for the writer of 'Schoolhouses, Primitive and Modern,' to be the 'Lizzie Lincoln' of 'The Republican.' I shared the genuine surprise of most of her fellow-students. We all knew 'Lizzie Lincoln's' poetry, but had not dreamed that she was one of our happy band. I remember how the blood crimsoned her face and neck as all eyes turned towards her, and what a new interest the familiar face had for me. I felt that, although we had all loved and respected, few of us had appreciated her at her real worth. She has found appreciation since in thousands of hearts and homes."

From the time of leaving the school in Bernardston her home was with her parents in Winchendon, and the years passed by, without any event of special interest, until her marriage, near the end of 1865. She was engaged in the duties of the family; **and,** being the eldest **of** the children, was helpful **as a daughter and** sister. At times her life was varied by occupation in **a** millinery store, and perhaps in other employment. **During all these years she** was a diligent and thoughtful reader, having access to a well-selected library which had been established in the village.

The following passages **from a letter of Rev. G. A.** Litchfield, formerly pastor of the Baptist church **in Winchendon,** gives his impression of her **character in** the closing years of her life. **He writes,** —

"I knew Mrs. Wakefield well for several years, and officiated both at her marriage and her funeral. I knew her in health and in sickness. I met her often in public, but oftener in the quiet of her maidenhood home, and later in that of her own home, when she had become the wife and mother. She was of a singularly modest and retiring nature. She always underrated her own ability.

"In presence of strangers she withdrew within herself; in presence of those whom she trusted as friends, she would often reveal her inner self, and charm the listener, not less by her characteristically original and imaginative mode of expression than by the choiceness of the thought expressed. . . . She was extremely happy in her use of language."

Mr. Litchfield then alludes to the fact that she had offers of assistance in extending her education, and states that it was a source of regret to those who knew her rare poetical genius, that her extreme self-distrust and dislike of notoriety induced her to decline all overtures of the kind. But there is reason to believe that other causes, highly creditable to her character, led to this decision. In one case a lady of wealth, with rare generosity, offered to give her a finished education, and wished to treat her as an adopted daughter; but, however desirable the literary advantages, she could not endure the thought of forming any connection that would come between herself and the loved ones of her own home. She chose wisely; and her heart had its reward in the love of her nearest kindred, and, later, in the cherished affection of husband and children. How much her heart was bound up in the little ones is apparent from the two poems which will be found in the division entitled "Love and Friendship." One is headed "Baby asleep," and the other, "Christmas Stockings." These were found by Mr. Wakefield, after her decease, written carelessly in pencil, as if under sudden impulse of the heart. Another piece was found by him enclosed in an envelope, and reserved for his own eye, after she was gone. It is entitled "A Fancy," and is a priceless legacy to a bereaved husband. One verse is among the most touching in the language; and the thought seems to have escaped expression hitherto, though it immediately finds an echo in all delicately tender souls : —

> " Forever in my quiet grave
>> (Albeit they say the dead
> Know nothing of the busy world
>> That whirls above their head),
> I think my sleep would be less deep
>> If any but thine own
> Were the last earthly touch I felt
>> *Ere I was left alone.*"

The whole poem bears witness to the happiness of her married life.

Nothing more needs to be said of her life, except to refer briefly to her last days. Mrs. C. P. Fairbanks, an intimate friend of Mrs. Wakefield, wrote to me, a few weeks after her decease, stating some items of interest : —

"She did not expect to get well, but she said nothing about the future. The day she died she seemed very cheerful. After she could not speak, she frequently smiled. Her sister asked her if it was her happy thoughts that made her smile so often. She bowed to her, and looked at her and smiled, so that her sister was fully satisfied. No one who has known her for the last few years has any doubts but she was a Christian. . . . You know we always called her very plain ; but in death her face was beautiful, and still she looked perfectly natural. I never can understand how it could be. On her pale brow, with reverent hands and tearful eyes, I twined the laurel wreath, and folded the 'pulseless hands,' and gently laid her down for that dreamless sleep which knows no waking, — more beautiful in death than ever I had seen her in life, — and to-day I mourn her loss as the dearest friend I ever had.   There is none that can ever fill her place; but there is light and hope 'just beyond the veil.' There is a new attraction 'over the river.'"

The memory of "Nancy Priest" is still kept as green as on the day of her death in many "hearts and homes," outside as well as within the bounds of the family circle; and the mention of her name calls up tender and grateful feelings in thousands of bereaved ones, who have derived consolation and strength in their griefs, from her best-known poem, "Over the River." Notices of the press, private letters, and oral communications, in great number, have expressed the general sorrow for her early departure, and the warmest sympathy with her stricken friends.

This imperfect Memoir may be fitly closed by the following extract from an article in "The Congregationalist," dated Nov. 3, 1870 : —

OVER THE RIVER.

"Our readers will have noticed that Mrs. Wakefield (who wrote the beautiful lines with the above-named title) has recently passed away by death. As nearly as we recollect the facts, these lines were first published to the world some fifteen years ago; and, what is remarkable in them, they have such a charm for the people as to keep them in constant circulation ever since. It may be doubted whether a single week has transpired, in the last ten years, when these verses might not have been picked up from one or more of our American newspapers in their issue of that week. We know, indeed, of no bit of poetry of late, from any pen, that has struck the popular mind so exactly. This is due, in a measure, to the facts that death is ever busy in these human households; and little children, in all their early brightness and beauty, are constantly passing out of their earthly to their heavenly home : and these lines contain the very balm of consolation for such wounded and bleeding hearts. But, aside from the subject-matter (for that is common to a great multitude of little poems in our language), there is in this a glory of conception, a beauty of language and of imagery, a burning glow of genius, such as are altogether remarkable."

RELIGIOUS POEMS.

OVER THE RIVER.

Over the river they beckon to me,

Loved ones who've crossed to the further

side;

The gleam of their snowy robes I see,

But their voices are lost in the dashing tide.

There's one with ringlets of sunny gold,

And eyes the reflection of heaven's own blue;

He crossed in the twilight, gray and cold,

And the pale mist hid him from mortal view.

We saw not the angels who met him there;

The gates of the city we could not see;

Over the river, over the river,

My brother stands waiting to welcome me.

Over the river the boatman pale
  Carried another, the household pet ;
Her brown curls waved in the gentle gale, —
  Darling Minnie ! I see her yet.
She crossed on her bosom her dimpled hands,
  And fearlessly entered the phantom bark ;
We felt it glide from the silver sands,
  And all our sunshine grew strangely dark.
We know she is safe on the further side,
  Where all the ransomed and angels be ;
Over the river, the mystic river,
  My childhood's idol is waiting for me.

For none return from those quiet shores,
  Who cross with the boatman cold and
    pale ;
We hear the dip of the golden oars,
  And catch a gleam of the snowy sail ;

And lo! they have passed from our yearning

    hearts,

Who cross the stream and are gone for aye!

We may not sunder the veil apart

    That hides from our vision the gates of day;

We only know that their barks no more

    May sail with us over life's stormy sea;

Yet somewhere, I know, on the unseen shore

    They watch and beckon and wait for me.

And I sit and think, when the sunset's gold

    Is flushing river and hill and shore,

I shall one day stand by the water cold

    And list for the sound of the boatman's oar;

I shall watch for a gleam of the flapping sail;

    I shall hear the boat as it gains the strand;

I shall pass from sight with the boatman pale

    To the better shore of the spirit-land;

I shall know the loved who have gone before,
And joyfully sweet will the meeting be,
When over the river, the peaceful river,
The angel of death shall carry me.

[We doubt not, with the dear ones who welcomed her to the heavenly shore, she waits for the loved ones yet left behind. — MARVIN.]

THE SPIRIT-LAND.

Beautiful country! oh, when shall I see thee?
When will my sinning and wandering be o'er?
When shall my feet, wounded, earth-stained and
    weary,
  Bathe in the river that laves thy green shore?
Beautiful country! the land of the angels,
  When shall I reach, and wander no more?

Beautiful city! how long ere the portals
  Of thy pearly gates shall be opened to me?
When shall I join in the songs of immortals,
  Praising the love that has brought me to
    thee?

Beautiful city, bright home of the blessed!
When shall I stand by thy crystalline sea?

Earth's joys are sweet, but they lure me from duty;
Earth-loves are strong, but they bind like a
chain!
Sometimes my heart clings to life and earth's
beauty
With a wild yearning that grows into pain;
And I forget the bright glories that wait me
Over the river on heaven's happy plain.

There bloom the flowers that wither, ah never!
There live the loved ones who've passed from
my sight;
There ring the anthems that sound on forever;
There walk the saints in their garments of
white;

There from God's throne floweth life's crystal
   river ;
  There shines the day that will end not in
   night.

Beautiful city, sweet rest for earth's weary !
  When will life's pilgrimage journey be o'er ?
Beautiful country ! ah, when shall I see thee ?
  When shall I stand on thy evergreen shore ?
Beautiful gate ! through thy opening portals,
  When shall I enter, to pass forth no more ?

SHALL WE KNOW EACH OTHER THERE?

WHEN we meet in fields elysian,
   Freed from this world's pain and care,
Shall we, with our spirit vision,
   See and know each other there?
Can it be that death will sever
   All life's dearest, holiest ties;
Do we look farewell forever
   When we close these mortal eyes?

Shall we in their angel plumage
   Know the loved of many years?
Lips that smiled when we were happy,
   Eyes that wept for all our tears?

Ah, how drear would be e'en heaven
  Did not hope, with glances bright,
Whisper that the hearts now riven
  In that world shall re-unite!

As we know the lambs we tended,
  When they came from pastures chill,
Bleating to the fold for shelter
  From the bare and frosty hill,
By the ribbon red or azure,
  That we tied long months before,
And we lift the gates with pleasure
  To receive them home once more, —

So shall they who've gone before us
  Ope for us the gate of light;
Kiss away our fears and trembling,
  Put on us the robe of white;

Lead us through the pastures vernal,

By the feet of angels trod,

To the stream of life eternal,

Flowing from the throne of God.

HEAVEN.

Beyond these chilling winds and gloomy skies,
    Beyond Death's cloudy portal,
There is a land where beauty never dies
    And love becomes immortal.

A land whose light is never dimmed by shade
    Whose fields are ever vernal,
Where nothing beautiful can ever fade,
    But blooms for aye eternal.

We may not know how sweet its balmy air,
    How bright and fair its flowers;

We may not hear the songs that echo there
Through those enchanted bowers.

The city's shining towers we may not see
With our dim, earthly vision ;
For Death, the silent warder, keeps the key
That opes those gates elysian.

But   sometimes,   where   adown   the   western
sky
The fiery sunset lingers,
Its golden gates swing inward noiselessly,
Unlocked by silent fingers.

And while they stand a moment half ajar,
Gleams from the inner glory
Stream lightly through the azure vault afar,
And half reveal the story.

O land unknown! O land of love divine!

   Father all-wise, eternal,

Guide, guide these wandering way-worn feet of

   mine

   Unto those pastures vernal.

THE ANGEL AND THE MAIDEN.

As I rested under the greenwood-tree,

The angel Azrael came to me;

He said, "The Eden land is fair;

Thou art weary of earth, — shall I waft thee

    there?"

But, though I had longed for the grave's still bed,

My spirit sank with a nameless dread;

I could not motion, I could not speak, —

The spirit was willing, the flesh was weak.

"I hoped," he said, "to have seen thee wear

The conqueror's crown on thy flowing hair;

I hoped to have given thee a golden lyre,

And heard thy voice in the heavenly choir."

But thou art weak and of mortal birth,

And thou clingest yet to the things of earth;

And longer still must thou tarry here,

Ere thou art fit for a higher sphere.

Yet look, O maiden, thine eyes shall see

A glimpse of the land of purity,

That thy soul may turn from these glittering
    toys

To the crystal fountain of purer joys.

Then the pale mist parted before my view,

And I saw the skies that are ever blue;

I caught a glimpse of the valleys green

And the river of life that floweth between;

I saw the gate to the realms of light;

I saw the choir in their robes of white,

And the gleam of the city's golden spires,

Like the glimmering lights of a thousand fires;

And I heard such music, so rich and clear,

As never fell on a mortal ear;

For one more note of that dulcet strain

I'd live a lifetime of care and pain.

Then mist spread slowly before the scene;

It hid the skies, and the valleys green;

The song of a bird on the still air broke;

The angel left me, and I — awoke.

THE EVENING LESSON.

Come to my knee, my darling!
  The long summer day is done;
And low to his rest in the crimson west
  Sinketh the fiery sun.
Come, and we'll watch together
  To see the first star appear,
And I'll tell you a beautiful story:
  Listen, and you shall hear.

Shall I tell you of wicked "Bluebeard,"
  Or of merry "Robin Hood"?
Of the wonderful "Lamp of Aladdin,"
  Or the hapless "Babes in the Wood"?

Nay, my darling knows them already:

She wishes for something true;

So I'll tell her a sweet, strange story,

Old, yet forever new.

Once, in the past's dim ages,

In a country far away,

On just such a starlit night as this,

An Infant in slumber lay.

But not in a costly cradle

Was the Baby hushed to rest;

Not on a downy pillow

Was his pure white forehead pressed.

It was a dismal stable;

Nestled upon the hay,

In a dark and narrow manger,

The new-born Infant lay;

And his mother stood beside him
And watched him with tender eyes,
While the patient cattle stood around
And looked their mute surprise.

And yet this lowly Infant
Was the Lord of heaven and earth ;
And angels came from the shining choir
To sing the Redeemer's birth ;
And shepherds from plains of Judah,
And wise men from afar,
Came with gifts to the holy Child,
Led on by a guiding star.

Now in the highest heaven,
Glorious all thought above
He liveth and reigneth ever,
And his holiest name is Love.

Love him and trust him, darling;
  Go to him every day;
Tell him your childish troubles
  In your own childish way.

What! is my darling weary?
  Her eyes are closing in sleep;
Over the orbs of shining blue
  Slowly the white lids creep;
Lower yet on my shoulder
  Droopeth her golden head;
Take her carefully, father,
  Carry her to her bed.

HOPE AND WAIT.

Why murmur, helpless child of fate,
For what a Father's hand denies?
Why upward to the crystal gate
Send thy weak moans and feeble cries?

Take heart! beneath the winter snows
The flowers of summer nestle warm,
And God's eternal sunshine glows
Unchanged above the darkest storm.

And, though life's wayside flowers be few,
And thorns thy tender feet may tear,

His hand can guide thee safely through,
And he will give thee strength to bear.

Look upward! though thy tear-dimmed eyes
May fail to pierce those clouds of night,
Behind those gloomy, frowning skies
The stars still burn serenely bright.

Stand, as of old all Israel stood
Before the widely parted sea;
His arm controls the mighty flood,
And He will give thee victory.

So shall the cypress on thy brow
Be changed into the conqueror's palm;
And life, one dismal dirge-note now,
Swell to a grand thanksgiving psalm.

OUR SHEPHERD.

Our Shepherd's watchful care
His flock shall safely keep;
To living pastures, green and fair,
His hand shall guide His sheep.

His gentle voice they know;
They follow where He leads,
Through vales where life's bright waters flow,
And over verdant meads.

But fly earth's rude alarms
And sin's alluring snares;

Safe folded in His loving arms
The tender lambs He bears.

He keeps them by His side;
Their souls to Him are dear;
He is their Father, Friend and Guide,
While they are wandering here.

And when life's day is o'er,
And rest and peace are given,
Bright angels on Death's farther shore
Shall welcome them to heaven.

LIFE.

"Life is a masquerade."

LIFE is *not* a masquerade!

There are hearts that can be trusted,

Hearts by selfishness unswayed,

Hearts that avarice has not rusted,

Hearts that love and cherish truth,

Deeming it no idle story,

Hearts that keep the dew of youth

When the head with age is hoary.

Life is not a masquerade!

Love is not a vague ideal;

Spite of all that knaves have said,

   Honest friendship still is real.

Let us not life's burden spurn;

   Gladly, bravely let us take it;

We have yet this truth to learn,

   Life is ever what we make it.

We may make it grand and pure,

   Though our lot be low and humble,

Building names that will endure

   When the pyramids shall crumble.

To the peaceful, heavenly plains

   We may draw, each moment, nigher,

Making sorrows, cares and pains

   Stepping-stones to raise us higher.

Let us, one united host,

   Forward press like friends and brothers;

Those whom God has blessed the most
  Doing most to bless the others.
So shall life become more sweet;
  So shall peace and joy be given;
So shall light to guide our feet
  Shine upon our path to heaven.

LINES ON MY LAST BIRTHDAY.

EIGHTEEN to-day! how swiftly time has sped
  On his aërial flight! how silently
The days and weeks and months away have fled,
  Bearing me forward on life's stormy sea,
Bearing me farther from those sunny hours
    When life seemed bright, and buttercups and
      daisies
I thought the fairest of the countless flowers
  That gemmed the fields or wildwoods' devious
    mazes!

Alas! that childhood hours return no more,
  Those golden moments of the happy mind,

When wealth and fame seem dancing on before,

  And every gloomy shadow falls behind!

But, as we near the summit of life's hill,

  The sweet-voiced sirens lure us on no more,

And as tales to the churchyard still

  The ever-lengthening shadows fall before.

Alas for childhood's fairy dreams of hope!

  Alas that they were naught but an ideal!

That we must dash aside her pleasant cup

  To drain the bitter chalice of the Real.

And yet the heart grows stronger with each trial;

  And e'en the bitter conflict in the soul,

Each thrill of pain, each hard, stern self-denial,

  May help us on towards the spirit-goal.

And yet to poet-minds how dark and dreary

  This rough and thorny path of life appears!

How oft, with eyes unstrung and spirits weary,
   They wander through this world of sighs and
      tears !
Too soon they feel the chilling world's cold
      censure,
   The heartless flattery or the smile of scorn ;
See others walk in ease, peradventure
   Their own torn feet too sharply feel the
      thorn.

But while I know not what my life may be,
   Or where my weary life-bark may be driven,
Father of light, I look alone to Thee
   To guide it safely to the destined haven !
If storm-tossed on the surging sea of life,
   The waif of every wave my boat shall be,
Breathe Thou upon the tempest and the strife,
   Or take the restless wanderer home to thee.

"A STILL, SMALL VOICE."

"A STILL, small voice," how oft we hear its
pleading,
Renewed from day to day,
And turn away, all careless and unheeding,
Refusing to obey!

It comes sometimes at the calm hour of twi-
light, —
That whisper in the breast;
Sometimes it waits the solemn hush of mid-
night,
And robs us of our rest.

It speaks, perhaps, of promises we've broken,
  Of bright hopes we have killed;
Of words of kindness we have left unspoken,
  And duties unfulfilled;

Of some weak brother, fallen now past hoping,
  Whose feet we might have stayed;
Some erring sister in the darkness groping,
  To whom we gave no aid.

Anon, it utters words of solemn warning, —
  "Repent, believe, obey;"
And we resolve, but with the light of morning
  We put such thoughts away.

Oh, hear the voice! oh, heed its earnest pleading
  While there are time and room,
Lest, at the last, upon thy ear unheeding
  It peal, the trump of doom.

JUDGE NOT.

"Judge not thy brother," Christ has said,
"Lest on thy own unworthy head
The wrath thou heap'st on him be shed."

But we forget the mandate stern;
And, if his feet from duty turn,
We let our wrath against him burn.

And, spurning pity's gentle sway,
We haste to tear each screen away,
And drag his errors to the day.

Not so does God's sweet mercy flow;
His vilest creatures here below
His pitying care and kindness know.

His blessed air is free to all ;

On good and evil, great and small,

He makes his glorious sunshine fall.

And, looking from His holy hill,

He marks the strivings of our will,

Knows all our sins, and loves us still.

But we who can so little know

From whence our brother's actions flow,

What thorns along his pathway grow, —

His helpless groping in the night,

His heartfelt struggles toward the light, —

We judge, and call on God to smite.

Ah ! much I fear that in that day

When all deceit is swept away,

And all things seen in Heaven's pure day,

If we have slighted this command,

And stretched not forth the friendly hand,

To help a feeble brother stand,

God's wrath — a black and heavy pall —

On our defenceless heads shall fall,

And we in vain for mercy call.

POEMS OF LOVE AND FRIENDSHIP.

TO MY HUSBAND.

Wʜᴇɴ that last change that comes to all
  Shall o'er my features spread;
When from my eyes life's light fades out,
  And from my cheeks the red;
When o'er the heart that once beat warm
  The pulseless hands you fold,
Oh, kiss my faded lips, beloved,
  Albeit they are cold!

For since the time when our two lives
  Together blent in one,
Like streams that from two different springs
  Flow singing into one,

No matter what of hope or light
  The weary day might miss,
I never close my eyes at night
  Without thy good-night kiss.

Forever in that quiet grave
  (Albeit they say the dead
Know nothing of the busy world
  That whirls above their head),
I think my sleep would be less deep
  If any but thine own
Were the last earthly touch I felt
  Ere I was left alone.

Kiss me, but do not weep, beloved!
  Nay, rather bless our God
That made so bright the little time
  That we together trod;

And doubt not that I love thee still

Wherever **I may** be,

That as in life each pulse that beats

Is true as steel to thee.

And think, that just beyond the veil

Within another home,

With love, **and** faith that ne'er shall fail,

I'll wait for thee to come.

BABY ASLEEP.

Baby has gone to the land of dreams.

Hush, or you'll wake him! how still it seems!

Carefully shut the bedroom door;

Noiselessly tip-toe across the floor.

See how sweet he looks as he lies

With fringed lids shutting the dark-brown eyes;

One pink palm pressing the dimpled cheek

And his red lips parted as if to speak.

Yonder in the low rocking-chair

Is a broken plaything, — he left it there;

And there, in the corner beside the door,

Lies a motley heap of many more, —

Jack-knife, picture-book, marbles, ball,

Tailless monkey and headless doll,

And new, bright pennies, his special joy,

By the father hoarded to please his boy.

There lie his shoes on the kitchen-floor

That all day long they have pattered o'er,

Battered and chubby, short and wide,

Worn at the toe, and cracked at the side;

And there hangs the little dress he wore,

Scarlet flannel, and nothing more;

But there clings about it a nameless charm,

For the sleeves are creased by his dimpled arm.

Dear little feet that are now so still,

Will ye ever walk in the paths of ill?

Rosebud lips, will ye ever part,

Bringing pain to a mother's heart?

Keep, O Father, that baby brow

Ever as pure from stain as now!

Lead him through life, by Thy guiding hand,

Safely into the better land!

THE CHRISTMAS STOCKINGS.

THERE they are in the corner,

Hanging up side by side, —

Four little, dainty stockings,

  Chubby and short and wide, —

One for Etta and Charlie,

  And one for shy little Nell';

And the wee little sock of crimson

  Belongs to the baby, Bell.

Bell, to whose infant beauty

  Every new day adds charms,

Taking no thought of the morrow,

  Sleeps in her mother's arms,

But up in their own little chamber,

Bright, eager eyes, I know,

Watch for the sledge by reindeers drawn

Over the crispy snow.

Sweet, simple faith of childhood!

Why should I break the spell?

Why should I tell them that only a myth

Is the "saint" they love so well?

Let them cherish a little longer

Their simple nursery lore:

There is time to learn worldly wisdom

In the future that lies before.

But what shall I put in the stockings?

For with morning's earliest light

I shall hear on the stairs the patter

Of tiny feet, bare and white;

And happy and childish voices,

Ringing childlike and clear,

Will chirrup a "Merry Christmas"

In a half-awakened ear.

There are books for the thoughtful Etta,

And pictures for sunny-haired Nell,

And skates and mittens for Charlie,

And toys for the baby, Bell.

As I drop them into the stockings,

My heart goes up with a prayer,

That the loving and tender Saviour

May make our darlings His care.

"Keep them, I pray Thee, ever

Safe in the narrow way;

Never in paths forbidden

Suffer their feet to stray.

Guard them and guide them, Jesus

And, if the world grows cold,

Gather them, faithful Shepherd,

Into Thy blessed fold."

HATTIE.

When Memory turns with trembling fingers
　　The misty pages of the past,
Aud fondly, sadly, fancy lingers
　　O'er hopes and dreams too bright to last,
Then let these simple lines remind thee,
　　While drifting o'er life's stormy sea,
Where'er its drifting tide may find me,
　　That there is one heart cares for thee.

And may my Muse's humble token
　　Remind thee of some happy hours,
Of girlhood's friendship still unbroken,
　　When comes the gloom of darker hours;

And if my life is one of care,

   And I a wanderer o'er life's sea,

Still this shall be my daily prayer,

   That only sunshine rest on thee.

LAST WORDS.

She said, "Why should we start and shrink?
  Why fall your tears in showers?
Heaven's land lies nearer than we think
  Unto this world of ours, —
So very near, that I can hear
  Its rivers softly flowing,
And feel its blessed atmosphere
  Upon my forehead blowing.

"When April danced upon the lea,
  With violets on her bosom,
I said, 'I shall not live to see
  The hay-time violets blossom.'

But God's own kind and loving way
    'Tis time alone discloses;
I thought ere May to pass away,
    Yet here I clasp June roses.

"So gently ebbs my life away,
    I marvel you can sorrow;
The eyes that oped on earth to-day
    Shall ope in heaven to-morrow;
For at the going of the night
    I heard a spirit warning,
'Look, yonder breaks the rosy light
    Of your last earthly morning.'

"Your love has given my life its charm,
    Through all my being flowing;
But stronger, tenderer is the arm,
    To whose kind care I'm going.

To bear me over Jordan's tide

God sends his strong evangel."

She ceased. Our home had lost its pride,

But heaven had gained an angel.

A PICTURE.

She sits in the twilight dim and tender,
  Carelessly folding her small white hands,
Watching the sunset's crimson splendor
  Fade from the broad, green meadow-lands, —

While the sweet south wind, like one that
    blesses,
  Kisses the forehead pure and fair,
Wooes the red lips with soft caresses,
  Daintily toys with the golden hair.

Softly the mantle of evening closes
  Over the landscape wide and fair;

Faintly the breath of the summer roses
  Comes on the dewy twilight air.

Still she sits by the window lonely,
  Gazing out, though the night grows dark;
While her thoughts — winged rovers — are following only
  The outward course of a gallant bark.

One that she loves as she loves none other,
  One she has loved this many a day
Better than father, better than brother,
  Sailed this morn in the ship away.

So she heeds not the wind's caressing;
  She is standing again on the wave-washed shore;

She feels his kiss and his whispered blessing,
   And is thinking his last words o'er and
     o'er :—

"When the steps of another summer
   Brighten the meadow and wood and shore,
Close on the steps of the fairy comer,
   I will return to roam no more."

"To roam no more;" and her thoughts run
     forward
   (It seems so long, but 'twill come so soon),
And bask in the blissful radiance borrowed
   From the rosy light of the next year's
     June.

Ah, she shudders! a quick suggestion
   Chills her heart to its inmost core:

She is asking herself the dreadful question,

"What if his ship should return no more?"

The clock strikes one: in dreams she hears it.

What can have changed the scene so soon?

For the wind wails now like a restless spirit,

And dark clouds drift o'er the rising moon.

Ay, weep, fond dreamer! for ere the morning,

Dark and stormy, shall dawn on thee,

He will have gone beyond returning

Over Death's dim, unsounded sea.

SCHOOL–CHILDREN.

They are passing now, a merry group: I can

hear each joyous tone.

Two are walking with close-clasped hands, and

one trips onward alone;

And each one holds in her dimpled hand a bunch

of spring flowers just blown.

One has eyes of the brightest blue, and curls

of the sunniest gold;

Lips like rosebuds, and brow white as the Parian

marble cold, —

Nellie, sweet darling, and pet of all! she is

only three Aprils old.

One has eyes of a darker hue, and hair like the
  raven's wing:
She could not move with a queenlier grace were
  she child of a sceptred king.
You should see her lip curl with scorn at some
  cruel or wicked thing.

And here is another boisterous troop of bare-
  footed, laughing boys,
Quick to share in each other's griefs, and smile
  at each other's joys:
Their teachers had need to be a second Job to
  bear with their fun and noise.

They are past; but my heart has followed them
  where my feet have been before:
I look back through the weary years, and I am
  a child once more,—

Through the shady path where the May pinks

grew to the low red schoolhouse door.

Oh, those pleasant walks through the grand old

woods, where the south wind tossed our

curls !

And the dew on the grass on the sunlight shone,

like strings of the ocean pearls.

Ah! the happiest of our lives were then, when

we were but careless girls !

Careless and happy! our hearts were glad as the

streamlet that ripples by ;

We shook the bee from the clover-bloom, and

followed the butterfly ;

And the squirrel peeped from his nest in the

tree, and chirped as we hurried by.

Widely and far are parted now: severed are
    friendship's bands;
Some are away in the distant West, and some
    in other lands;
Some dear eyes we have closed in rest, and
    folded some weary hands.

We turn again to those early days when the
    path grows before,
And we cry again aloud, "Come back again, O
    halcyon days of yore!"
And they send but a doleful requiem back, the
    echo of "Never more."

APRIL RAIN.

Patter, patter, comes down the rain:
  Small are the drops, but they fall right fast,
Melting the snow on the frozen plain
  Where the stern king of the North has passed.
Dashing and spattering over the pane,
Patter, patter, comes down the rain.

The wind is rough, and the leaden sky
  Blusters and frowns at the frozen earth;
Over the heavens the gray clouds fly,
  And the firelight flickers upon the hearth.
But I heed not the storm, I hear not the blast;
For Memory is roaming over the Past.

Among the things she loveth best

  Are friends of childhood, — a bright-eyed

    band :

Some are away in the distant West,

  And some have passed to the spirit-land ;

And yet, when the voice of Memory calls,

They are living pictures on Time's gray walls.

Some whom I loved in the days of yore,

  Absence and time have sadly changed ;

Some whom I shrine in my heart no more, —

  Some (oh, saddest of all) estranged,

Whose very names make a thrill of pain

As surely as sunshine follows the rain.

Then my thoughts go out to the churchyard

    old ;

  And the tall, white tombstones again I see,

And, shuddering, think how damp and cold
  Must the narrow bed of the sleepers be.
But, oh! if they feel not care and pain,
Will they start at the drops of the April
    rain?

Then I list again to the moaning breeze
  As it laughs and sighs through the waving
    es,
And gaze far out through the poplar-trees,
  Where the cheerful glow of the lamp-light
    shines.
Oh the saddest spot where the feet may
    tread
Is over the heart's "unburied dead"!

Old bygone memories, why come ye back
  With the sighing wind and pattering rain?

All vain and wild are these yearnings deep,

And I crush them down in my heart again,

And patient wait through the long, dark night,

For the radiant beams of the morning light.

BE KIND.

Be kind to each other;
For little ye know
How harsh words embitter
Life's hours with woe;
They leave a dark shadow
Of bitter regret,
And harsh words spoken
Ye cannot forget.

Be kind to each other
In life's sunny hours,
For kindness will cover
Life's pathway with flowers;

Be gentle, be patient,

And peace, like a dove,

Shall dwell with thee ever, —

Sweet peace from above.

"TELL THEM I AM NO MORE."

TELL them I am no more!
Tell them life's fitful fever-dream is o'er;
Tell them its brittle chain is only riven
To be reclasped in heaven.

Tell them I longed to go,
To leave this world's cold heartlessness and
    show,
To bow with the adoring cherubim,
And tune my harp to Him.

Tell them that my young life
Was darkly shadowed o'er by care and strife;

Life's little time-voyage is but short at best;
Heaven has a safer rest.

Tell them the world was cold,
And the good Shepherd brought me to the fold;
There in green pastures, by His kind hand led,
"I live, whom ye call dead."

Tell them to mourn not much;
My spirit shrank from the cold tempest's touch,
As the mimosa at the touch of blight
Folds up its petals bright.

ESTRANGEMENT.

We have been friends together in the happy
days of yore;
We've spent together sunny hours that come
again no more;
And we meet as passing strangers in the gay
and heartless crowd,
With dark averted faces, or with glances cold
and proud.
There is no flush upon the cheek, no light
within the eye,
As when in days forever gone each knew the
other nigh.

Oh, wherefore should this anger-cloud veil heart
and cheek and brow?

We have been friends together: shall a light
word part us now?

We have been friends together; my hand has
lain in thine.

I've gazed into thy earnest eyes, and they have
answered mine;

Together in the twilight we have watched the
first star gleam,

And our hearts were blent together like the
currents of a stream.

Oh, it was but a little thing that turned our
barks apart, —

Light, careless words, that wounded though they
came not from the heart;

And still at the same spirit-shrine we both in
secret bow;

We have been friends together : shall a light
     word part us now?
Oh, look not down so sternly with thy darkly
     shadowed eyes !
I do not need thine anger-cloud to darken life's
     dark skies, —
We have been friends together ; let us be
     friends again :
It is not well to tread alone life's path of care
     and pain ;
And, as thou hopest at the last to gain a glori-
     ous heaven,
Forgive my wayward wanderings, as thou wouldst
     be forgiven ;
Look kindly on me once again, as in the days
     of yore, —
We have been friends together : shall we not be
     friends once more?

WANDERINGS AND THOUGHTS ON A SUMMER DAY.

We wandered down the garden-walks,
  And talked of all indifferent things;
We watched the mating swallows' flight,
Swifter than pencil-rays of light:
  She said, "Ah, would that I had wings!"

And I replied, "Wish not for wings,
  My angel, lest I lose thee quite;
Even now I sometimes fear to see
Thee fading into vacancy,
  Or melting slowly into light."

"Am I a child, then, still," she cried,
  "That you should deal in childish speech?
Methinks you overact your part;
Believe me, a true woman's heart
  Stale flattery can never reach."

We wandered 'neath the forest shade,
  And where around the giant tree
The ivy's twining fingers strayed.
"Ah! wouldst thou cling to me," I said,
  "Thus would I joy to shelter thee."

And she replied, "Compare not me
  To yonder weak and clinging vine;
Should the red lightning cleave the tree,
So strong and beautiful to see,
  Where then would the poor ivy twine?

"Grovelling upon the dusty earth,
　　And bruised by feet of passers-by,
Devoid of beauty and of grace,
　　It could but live a little space,
　　　Then droop and wither, fade and die."

CROSSING THE RIVER.

"IT is growing dark," she murmured; "and my

heart beats faint and slow;

Chilly dews are gathering slowly, — gathering

on my cheek and brow.

I can scarcely hear the rustle of the trembling

aspen-tree,

And the raindrops falling gently, gently falling

over me;

But I hear low voices murmur, — voices as the

zephyrs sweet, —

While the cold waves of the Jordan lave my

weary, earth-tired feet.

"Come, and sit beside me, mother; come, and
    put your hand in mine;
Look with me on yonder lakelet, where the
    glancing sunbeams shine,
While I tell you of a vision, beautiful and
    strangely bright,
That I saw before me, mother, in the watches
    of the night.
Do you not remember, mother, 'twas a glorious
    day of spring,
When the violets were in blossom, and the
    larks began to sing,
That my father and my brother sailed from
    home and friends away,
And we watched the noble vessel gliding
    swiftly down the bay?

"Then the long and weary hours, lengthening
    into days and weeks,

When distress and painful waiting drove the
        health-tints from your cheeks ;
Then — how well can I remember ! — came the
        tidings of the gale :
‘Lost at sea, and all hands perished, — not a
        soul to tell the tale.’
Then the days of utter darkness, dragging
        painfully along,
When our hearts could hardly listen to our pet
        canary’s song,
And my heart rebelled and murmured, — mur-
        mured at His holy will, —
And the tempest waves of feeling scarcely
        were a moment still.

“But last night, as I lay tossing restlessly upon
        my bed,
With the anguish at my heartstrings, and the
        pain that racked my head,

All the room grew dim with shadows; with a
    slow, upheaving motion

Rose they like the angry surges of the blue
    and storm-tossed ocean.

Slowly from the misty vapors rose a phantom
    pale and fair,

With the dripping seaweed clinging closely to
    his clustering hair;

And another, — taller, paler, with a forehead
    marred by time, —

And about them glowed the radiance of that
    unseen, perfect clime.

" Brighter, brighter grew the halo, till my eyes
    could scarce behold;

And methought these naked rafters looked like
    bars of solid gold,

And the hands of that old dial glittered with a
    diamond ray :

All around our cheerless chamber shone the
    radiant glow of day.
Then the veil was taken from me, and I knew
    our spirit-guests, —
They who sleep where Ocean mutters her deep
    requiem o'er their breasts ;
And I trembled with vague terror, scarcely
    daring e'en to speak,
Lest a sound or look or motion that celestial
    spell should break.

" 'Weep no more, beloved daughter,' — 'twas
    my father's voice that spoke ;
Sweeter than the sweetest music on my listen-
    ing ear it broke, —
'Weep no more, for we are happy ; yet a little
    longer wait,
And our happy band shall greet you at the
    broad and shining gate.'

Then the golden halo faded, and the room was
    dark again;
But within my heart was gladness, where before
    were grief and pain;
And the blessed words he uttered fell upon
    my soul like balm:
So the tempest has subsided, and my weary
    mind is calm.

"I shall meet them" — But death's angel
    stooped upon his shadowy wing,
And the loved one gladly followed to the land
    where angels sing.
Silently, as stars at midnight sink within the
    western skies,
Welled the light of angel glory in the depths
    of those blue eyes;
But the soul was climbing higher than the
    sunbeam or the star,

To the great white throne above us, where the
     souls of just ones are.

Silently we moved about her; silently we
     smoothed her hair,

For a tearful awe was on us, for the steps of
     Death were there.

LINES TO L. L. H.

Do you remember, sister Lu,
  The little " willow lane"?
On either side the hedge, there stood
  Green fields of waving grain.
How many times we've wandered there,
  In summer's quiet hours,
As happy as the humming-bird
  That nestled in the flowers!

Have you forgot the maple-tree
  That grew so near the stream,
How, through its interlacing boughs,
  The sunlight used to gleam?

'Twas there the earliest violets grew,
  And there they lingered last :
I'm sure you've not forgotten, Lu,
  These " memories of the past."

How often in the forest, too,
  We wandered side by side,
In the happy days of "long ago,"
  Before you were a bride !
Never were skies so bright and blue,
  Or stars so clear and bright,
As the sky that arched above us then,
  And the stars that gemmed the night.

We are no longer children, Lu,
  And on life's battle-plain,
Where mingled oft in Pleasure's cup
  Are sorrow, care, and pain.

Sweet memories of the past will come,
  Like dew upon the flowers,
To keep alive the faith and hope
  Of childhood's sunny hours.

THE WAY OF THE WORLD.

I WONDER if poverty is a stain:
When I passed to-day by Anna Lee,
Her red lips curled with a proud disdain;
They wore no welcoming smile for me.

I was weak and foolish and vain, I know,
But my eyes grew misty and dim with tears:
I had measured her love by my own, and so
I had not dreamed it would change with
years.

Long years had passed since I saw her last;
The world has altered to her and me:

I on life's ocean am friendless cast,

And a petted heiress is Anna Lee.

Mid the hurrying crowd I took my stand,

And waited her coming with eager eye;

She gathered her silks in her dainty hand,

And coldly, haughtily passed me by.

Is it my fault that I am poor?

Is love to be bought and sold?

Have only the rich a right to life?

Must the chain of friendship be clasped with

gold?

You are flattered and worshipped, Anna Lee,

Till you almost fancy yourself divine;

But the time may come — ay, the time will be —

When you would not mock at a love like mine.

For youth and beauty will fleet and wane,

And friends will vanish when riches flee:

God grant you may never feel the pain

Your scorn and silence have given me!

REMEMBER THE ABSENT.

REMEMBER the absent! though long weary
miles
Stretch darkly between us, and cares
intervene;
Remember the pleasures of days that are gone,
And still keep their memory fadeless and
green.

Remember the absent! though others are
near,
And you dream that their friendship will
never grow cold;

Remember there's one holds your memory
dear,
And treasures it up as the miser his gold.

Remember the absent when music's sweet
tone
Is thrilling thy heart with a throbbing
delight!
Remember how often thy voice joined my own,
And our songs rang out clear on the star-
lighted night.

Remember the absent! though far, far away;
Remember amid every sorrow and care;
And, when in the twilight you bow you to
pray,
Remember the absent, and plead for me
there.

LINES WRITTEN TO HER SCHOOL-MATES.

E'ER many suns have risen and set,
   I leave my pleasant home
And friends and schoolmates with regret,
   Mid other scenes to roam ;
And now, while I am with you here,
   Sad thoughts my bosom swell,
That I must leave my home so dear,
   And say a sad farewell.

I may not see my home again
   For many, many years :

What wonder that I leave it then
  With sadness and with tears?
My home within the Granite State
  May even be as fair
As my home within the old Bay State;
  But my heart will not be there.

And I must bid you now farewell,
  New friends and home to find:
My mountain-home may be as fair,
  And other friends as kind;
But my heart will ever turn from it,
  In sorrow or despair,
To my home within the old Bay State,
  And friends that I left there.

Farewell! farewell! Heaven only knows
  When we shall meet again;

But we may hold sweet intercourse

Through the medium of the pen.

We have been friends, and though apart,

If feelings, thought, and will

Are still as now in unison,

We'll be together still.

ADDITIONAL LINES TO HER SCHOOL-MATES.

I'M going to leave the old Bay State,
   And my own dear, pleasant home,
To live a while mid other scenes,
   O'er other hills to roam.
My feet will press the verdant soil,
   With happy heart elate;
So I'm off, I'm off, on the wings of the wind
   To my home in the Granite State.

For tears and sighs I can spare no time;
   No vain regrets I feel:
It's the fate which fortune gave to me,
   And set with solemn seal.

For "sad farewells" I do not care,
And cannot for them wait ;
For I'm off, I'm off, on the wings of the wind
To my home in the Granite State.

So, friends, good-by : I cannot wait ;
But, if you chance to come
Within the Granite State, just call
And see me at my home.
The latch-string hangs outside the door :
To knock you need not wait ;
Now I'm off, I'm off, on the wings of the wind
To my home in the Granite State.

TOO LATE.

"Of all sad words of tongue or pen,
The saddest are these, 'It might have been.'"

Talk not to me of coldness or deceit;
Talk not to me of a remorseless fate:
There was a time when I had deemed it
    sweet
To be beloved by thee, but 'tis too late.

Once all the pulses of my heart were stirred
By the most careless mention of thy name:
Thy slightest glance, thy lightest spoken word,
Kindled my cheek with sunset's ruddy flame.

And then there dawned on thee a fairer face,
  And the shy, awkward child was soon forgot:
I had not charm of beauty or of grace
  To keep you mine, and so I murmured
    not.

Now, after all these years of wandering,
  When all the dreams of youth are gone to
    waste,
You come again, and in your heart you bring
  The cup I have no longer heart to taste.

You love me with your manhood's strength at
    last:
  I read untouched the secret in your eyes;
I might have loved you; but the time is
    past,
  And I—I do not wish it otherwise.

The love I longed for once is mine at last;
   I know it by a thousand silent signs:
By the dim light of my long-buried past,
   All that is in your heart my heart divines.

If but my hands rest lightly on your arm,
   Your strong frame trembles now as mine did
      then.
My cheeks blush not; my pulses beat on calm:
   You are to me no more than other men.

I can look back with eyes undimmed and clear,
   And forward with no wish to change my fate;
And if thou wilt, that once I held thee dear,
   Say not again, "It is too late."

ONE YEAR AGO TO-DAY.

I AM sitting in twilight
  To take my evening rest,
And watch the crimson sunset
  Fade slowly from the west.
On the wall the firelight flitters,
  And the shadows dance and play,
While my thoughts go travelling backwards
  To a year ago to-day.

I shut my eyes, and ponder,
  Till the present seems a dream :
In the gathering gloom and darkness
  I can see the white tents gleam ;

And the footstep of the passer,
  As it echoes down the street,
Becomes the sentry's footfall
  Pacing slowly down his beat.

My wife sits here beside me,
  And I hold her hand in mine;
But I'm listening for the drum-beat,
  And the tramping of the line;
And the voice sounds faint and distant,
  Like some far-off, unseen stream;
And I half expect the bugle
  To wake me from a dream.

Past and present, which is real?
  Is my country's peril past?
And the hour I scarce dared hope for,
  Is it truly mine at last?

Do I see a face beside me
  That I thought to see no more?
Or am I only dreaming,
  As a thousand times before?

ELEGIAC POEMS.

UNDER THE RIVER.

Thou blue Potomac, gently flow!
  Committed to thy keeping,
With hearts that quailed not 'neath the foe,
  My loved and lost is sleeping.
Ye little waves that kiss the light,
  Upspringing in your gladness,
I have a tale to tell to-night,
  Should tame you all to sadness.

But grief may come, and grief may go,
  And hearts meet, and hearts sever:
The sun shines on the stream's still flow,
  And so 'twill be forever.

Yet, thou blue river, as I sit
　And muse beside thee sadly,
I cannot bear that thou shouldst yet
　Smile on so warm and gladly:
I think of dear eyes that met mine,—
　Brave eyes, that smiled at parting.
Ah me! they've lost their gentle smile,
　And tears in mine are starting.

But grief may come, and grief may go,
　And hearts meet, and hearts sever:
The sun shines on, the stream's still flow,
　And so 'twill be forever.

Well, sparkle on! it boots not now:
　He heeds not; should I mind it?
But, oh! kiss gently his cold brow,
　Ye little waves that find it.

Kiss his white lips, as once I pressed
  My kisses warm and glowing,
And murmur gently round his rest,
  Ye bright waves, brightly flowing.

But grief may come and grief may go,
  And hearts meet and hearts sever:
The sun shines on the stream's still flow,
  And so 'twill be forever.

DOWN BY THE RIVER.

Madge and Nellie and Kate and I
  Wandered down by the river's side,
And watched the wavering shadows fly
  Like gliding barks o'er its level tide.

And many a merry song we sung,
  And many a joyous tale we told,
Till the air with our fitful laughter rung
  And the echo replied from the forest old.

Memory tells me that they were fair, —
  Madge, with her clustering nut-brown curls,

And Nellie and Kate with **their** sunny hair,
 And lips like rosebuds and teeth like **pearls.**

Rocking to rest in their sweet content,
 The birds their heaven-taught vesper sung;
And over our heads, like a gorgeous tent,
 The crimson curtains of sunset hung.

The lilies lifted their queenly **heads**
 And swayed with **the current to and fro;**
And the wild flowers leaned o'er their **grassy**
  beds
 And gazed at themselves in the wave below.

Now, as then, on the level tide
 The crimson stains of the sunset lie;
But we roam no more by the river's side, —
 Madge and Nellie and Kate and I.

I go alone to the churchyard gray,
  Where three white stones stand side by side;
And memory carries my thoughts away
  To the dismal day when our loved ones died.

Silently passed they, one by one,
  As stars fade out from the sky above
In the glorious beams of the rising sun:
  Ah, if death were the end of earthly love!

THE DYING GIRL'S LAST WISH.

Oh! bury me not in the dismal tomb,
Where all is coldness, stillness and gloom;
Let me rest in peace, when I must die,
Beneath the canopy of the sky.

Oh! place not over me lying stones
To mark the crypt of my mouldering bones;
But make my grave in some sunny spot
Where I may sleep by the world forgot.

And robe me not in a ghostly dress
When I am arrayed for my dreamless sleep;

When the sods of the valley my head shall

press,

And o'er me the bending willow sweep.

But strew ye with flowers my narrow bed,

And shed not a tear o'er my early rest;

But think, as ye pillow my youthful head,

'Tis the will of God: He knoweth best.

LINES WRITTEN ON THE DEATH OF MR. AND MRS. HALE.

Weep not; for Christians have gone home
To mansions in the sky;
To roam through fields of Paradise,
Where pleasures never die.

No care nor pain can e'er molest,
Nor troubles vex them more,
No sorrow break upon their rest:
Their mortal life is o'er.

Tearful and gentle in their lives,
Death had for them no pain;

The world had lost its power to charm,

For them to die was gain.

For they have gained a better land,

And death's dark stream is past;

And with the glorious angel-band

Their happy lot is cast.

HOME.

Tny home is sad and desolate: no father now
  is there

To greet thee with a welcome home; no
  mother's tender care

And sympathy to lighten thy every toil and
  pain,

And nevermore that much-loved voice shall
  greet thy ear again.

And never canst thou receive their blessings
  and their prayers:

Thy home is still unchanged, but, oh! the
  loved ones are not there;

And other feet will tread the paths that they
    so long have trod,
While their freed spirits gladly dwell before
    the throne of God.

Yet upward look, midst all thy grief and
    anguish and distress,
Unto the gracious Father of those who're
    fatherless ;
And think, oh, think! when thou art free from
    all life's care and pain,
In a world of ransomed spirits thou shalt
    meet them both again.

LITTLE EVA.

Part the damp curls from the forehead,
  For the spirit has flown to the skies;
Press down the darkly fringed eyelids
  Over the beautiful eyes;
Fold the white hands on her bosom;
  Place a white rose by her side:
Just as our darling one blossomed,
  Just so our darling one died.

Naught cares she now for our weeping:
  Tears like the raindrops may fall;
Calmly our Eva lies sleeping;
  Happiest is she of all.

Forth come ye now to behold her;
    Take a last look while you may;
Then to green, quiet churchyard,
    Bear on the beautiful clay.

Lower ye lightly her coffin;
    Press the green turf on her breast;
Then, 'neath the boughs of the willow,
    Leave we our Eva to rest.
What though our home may seem dreary?
    What though the tears fill our eyes?
Her tiny feet were earth-weary:
    Now she has gone to the skies.

Plant ye the locust-tree o'er her;
    There let the violet wave,
Every thing transient and lovely
    Grow o'er her tear-watered grave.

There let the first sunlight glimmer;

There let the last sunbeam rest,

And the pale, silent moon shine upon it,

Like a "smile from the land of the blest."

THE SOLDIER'S DEATH.

They bore him to a cool and grassy place,
  So motionless they almost deemed him
    dead;
And fanned with tender care the pallid face,
  And with pure water bathed his drooping
    head,
Till his eyes opened, and a languid smile
  Played round his dying lips; and, when he
    spoke,
They hushed their very breath to listen, while
  That low, faint murmur on the calm air
    broke.

"Comrades, my waning life is almost fled;

Death's dampness gathers on my brow and

cheek,

And from this gaping wound the bullet made

The crimson life-blood oozes while I speak.

I shall be resting quietly ere long,

And shall not need your love and tender care:

Your hearts are valiant, and your arms are strong,

Go back, my comrades! you are needed there.

"But bear me first to yonder grassy sod,

Whence I can turn my eyes upon the fight.

Gently, there! Leave me now alone with God,

And go you back to battle for the right."

Then his mind wandered; and the beating drum,

The roar of cannon, and the din of strife

Changed to familiar, far-off sounds of home,

Or sweet, low tones of mother, child, or wife.

And the receding battle's frequent shocks,
　　Softened by distance, coming on the breeze,
Seemed to him like the bleating of the flocks,
　　Or hiveward murmur of the laden bees;
Until there came a mighty shout at length,
　　A cry that rose and swelled to "Victory!"
And, opening his dim eyes with sudden strength,
　　He saw the foemen's ranks divide, and fly.

He rose; he sat erect in his own blood;
　　His heart throbbed joyfully as when a boy:
"They fly! they fly!" he cried, and up to God
　　His spirit passed on that last shout of joy.
And so they found him, when they sought him
　　　　there,
Lifeless and cold in that secluded place, —
　　The rigid fingers clasped as if in prayer,
And that last smile of triumph on his face.

APRIL DAISIES.

How many thoughts beyond her years,
That then were all unheeded,
We think of now with blinding tears, —
Sweet teaching that we needed!
Three happy years we led her feet
Among life's thorny mazes;
The fourth we laid her down to sleep
Beneath the April daisies.

'Tis well, and we are reconciled;
For He who gave the blossom,
Who lent to us our angel-child,
Recalled her to his bosom;

And, waiting till He calls for me
To sing with her His praises,
I keep her blessed memory
Embalmed in April daisies.

THE MESSENGER.

There came a messenger at early dawning,
    While yet the stars shone bright;
Unheralded by any sound or warning,
    He entered as of right.

I felt an awful shadow o'er the dwelling,
    And all my blood grew chill;
My heart, with awful expectation swelling,
    Throbbed once, and then stood still.

Through the dark hall with folded pinions
        gliding,
    And steps of noiseless tread,

He entered where our patient one lay wasting,
    And stood beside the bed.

The lamp burned dim; the clock that told the
    hour
    Rang like a funeral knell;
And from the roses, in a fitful shower,
    The red and white leaves fell.

He lingered till the shades of night were banished,
    And all the stars grew dim;
And, when at last the ghostly presence vanished,
    Our loved one went with him.

Ah, well! the days glide by us like a shadow,
    The years like moments flee;
Next time the messenger our threshold crosses,
    He'll come, perhaps, for me.

LITTLE NELLIE.

Fold the tiny dimpled hands
  On the bosom pure and fair;
Softly smooth the shining bands
  Of her dark and glossy hair.
It is hard to give her up,
  Young, and, oh, so passing fair!
Very bitter is the cup;
  Heavy is the grief to bear.

Two short summers closed her eyes,
  Of her home the life and light;
Now as still and cold she lies
  As a marble statue might.

Tears will all unheeded fall

    On her face for whom you weep;

And the name you vainly call

    Will not break her dreamless sleep.

Yet 'tis nothing but the form

    That you lay beneath the sod;

For, beyond earth's every storm,

    Little Nellie lives with God.

She is one of that vast throng

    That the nearest dwell to Him,

And she lisps the tuneful song

    Of the saints and cherubim.

Little Nellie, called so soon

    In thy childhood's sinless years,

Watch o'er us that linger on

    In this world of sin and tears;

For we know not whether late

  Or ere long our time shall be ;

Plead for us at Mercy's gate,

  That we soon may follow thee.

IN MEMORIAM.[1]

CAN this be death? It seems scarcely a min-
  ute
  Since these closed eyes looked fondly in my
  own,
And these pale lips, sealed with Death's icy
  signet,
  Spoke with their wonted, kind, familiar tone.
Look! even yet a smile upon them lingers,
  Like a radiance from the unseen land;
'Tis but a moment since these rigid fingers
  Returned the pressure of my clasping hand.

[1] Orville W. Priest died June 20, 1865.

Yet thou art gone. Vain is our bitter weeping:
  Tears fall unheeded on thy marble breast;
Our sorrow troubles not thy quiet sleeping;
  Our voices break not in upon thy rest.
Vain were the prayers of father or of mother;
  For a hand beckoned that we could not
    see:
Oh, had it been but possible, my brother,
  God knows how gladly I had died for thee!

How shall I miss thee! When around the table
  At eve we gather, who can fill thy place?
I shall glance up from poem or from fable
  To meet no answering smile upon thy face.
If at our lonely meals I raise my eyelids,
  I shall behold an ever-vacant chair:
At morning and at noontide and at evening,
  My brother, I shall miss thee everywhere.

Yet fare thee well! Thy young life fitly closes
  On the bright morning of this perfect day:
We lay thee down beneath the sweet June
    roses ;
  For thou wert pure and brief-lived, even as
    they.
Sleep sweet, our beloved! Much has been spared
    thee
  Of this world's conflicts, pain, and bitter woe,
And some time, in the land of the hereafter,
  Why thou wert taken from us we shall know.

IN MEMORIAM.

'Tis hard to see our loved ones die ;
  'Tis hard to watch the failing breath,
  To see the dear eyes close in death,
To speak and win no kind reply.

And well I know 'tis harder still
  To lay the precious form away,
  To moulder back to common clay,
And feel no rising of the will.

So, when to-day I stood before
  The coffin where your darling slept,
  I did not wonder that you wept,
For my own eyes were running o'er.

And yet I wept not for the dead!

How could I weep for one who stands

Among the shining angel-bands

With life's bright crown upon his head?

I wept for those who loved him so,

Whose life was in his being bound,

Whose very heartstrings bound around

The little form laid cold and low.

Ah, tender parents! while you weep

To-night above the tiny bed

Where rests no more the sunny head,

The angels hush him to his sleep.

And though life seems a weary load,

And home an empty, joyless place,

Without the sunshine of his face,

Can you not trust your child with God?

O mourning parents! dry your eyes,

And follow where his small white hand

Is beckoning upward to that land

Where love immortal never dies.

THE LOST CHILD.

They sought her in the field and grove,
Where'er they thought her feet might rove,
Exploring every nook and cove;

And down within the shady dell,
Where the wild lily hung its bell,
And filled the air with pleasant smell;

And where wild rose and ivy made
Alternate streaks of sun and shade,
And the light chestnut-tassels swayed.

And where the pale, sweet May pinks grew,
And violets opened eyes of blue,
Weeping bright drops of honey-dew.

But all in vain! Then some one said,

"The river winds along its bed,

Through meadows blossomed white and red, —

"Perhaps she has wandered there." All feet

Were turned this last retreat,

Where they might hope the child to meet.

And one along the river side,

On white sand left there by the tide,

The prints of tiny feet espied;

And stooping down with straining sight,

And eyes hand-shaded from the light,

Caught a faint gleam of something white.

He raised it with a trembling hand,

And drew it heavily to land,

And laid the dead child on the sand.

The blue eyes had a stony glare,
And the long, golden, curling hair
Lay dripping on the shoulders bare;

And in the tiny, dimpled hand
Wild violets of the meadow-land
Still by the rigid fingers spanned.

Then home the lifeless form they bore:
The mother met them at the door
Those pattering feet might cross no more.

And there were sobs and softening sighs,
And gushing tears from many eyes,
And whispered words and low replies.

The father sat like one amazed;
Nor once his heavy eyelids raised,
But ever on the pale corpse gazed;

And to the pastor's words of hope,

Replied, "I cannot give her up;

I cannot drink the bitter cup.

"God knows how dear she was to me,

My child, my darling Rosalie!

Oh, would that I were dead, like thee!"

Night came, — a night of cloudless calm,

With starry eyes and breath of balm;

But beauty had no power to charm.

Then with the dead hand in his own,

Whose touch was colder than the stone,

He bent the knee to pray alone.

And, lo! the clouds of grief were gone;

Faith once more triumphed on her throne:

Her full heart said, "Thy will be done!

" This form is nothing but the clay,

Through which my darling winged her way

To purer air and brighter day.

" What though the casket must decay?

The Lord hath given, and taken away:

Blest be his holy name for aye!"

Full on him shone the moonbeams fair,

And on the dead child's golden hair,

And rested like a halo there.

ELEGIAC LINES.

Sʜᴇ was too fair, too sweet a flower,[1]
  To live in a dark world like this;
Her heavenly Father took her home
  To his abode of purest bliss.

She wished to go: she longed to greet
  The loved and lost of other days,
To tune her voice in chorus sweet,
  And swell the ceaseless song of praise.

We cannot mourn, nor wish her back
  To tread life's path with us again;

[1] Laura Jane Johnson, aged eighteen years, nine months.

Her spirit longed to soar above:
'Twas sweet to live ; to die was gain.

Now she has gained a brighter land,
And death's cold stream is past ;
Hers are the joys at God's right hand,
That shall forever last.

THE SNOW.

How lightly and softly and pure it falls,
  Covering the earth with a mantle fair,
Robing even the brown stone walls
  With ermine a king might be proud to wear.
And the brave old evergreen trees that mark
The distant hills with their outline dark,
Whiter and whiter hourly grow,
Till they bend 'neath their weight of fleecy snow.

Sitting beside my window low,
  Through the flakes that fall like a curtain thin,
I watch the gradual growth of the snow
  O'er mounds where my last year's flowers have
    been ;

Growing and growing silently,

Till the bare, brown stalks are all I see, —

Stalks that beneath the sun and showers

Budded and burst into perfect flowers.

Then I think of a mound in the churchyard old,

　Where once in the spring time of long ago

A bud of beauty, all pale and cold,

　Was laid away 'neath the melting snow.

There were tears in my father's eyes that day,

And my mother sobbed o'er the beautiful clay;

Yet the mound over which my myrtle creeps

Is larger than that where my brother sleeps.

It was "only an infant," the neighbors said,

　As they gazed on the tiny features fair:

Could they dream of the light that fled

　With the little form that was sleeping there?

Happy .themselves, could they dimly guess
At the pride and beauty and loveliness,
The world-wide hope, and the springing joy,
That was buried up with the only boy?

Ah, well! I know that the spring will come,
  With its soft, blue skies, and its warm, glad
    showers;
And the birds will sing, and the bees will hum,
  And these bare, brown stalks will be gay with
    flowers:
So the little form that with tears and sighs
Was buried away from our mortal eyes,
Out of that narrow grave shall rise
To bloom in the garden of paradise.

OUR LILY.[1]

We had a little lily bud,

   A bud of promise rare,

A blessing from the hand of God:

   We treasured her with care.

'Twas joy to watch her infant mind,

   And teach her lips to speak:

We feared lest even heaven's wind

   Should roughly fan her cheek.

Two happy summers did her tiny feet

   Walk life's rough path with ours,

[1] Lines written for Mr. and Mrs. C. L. Carter on the death of their only daughter.

And then we laid her down to sleep
Beneath the fading flowers.

Oh! it was hard to give her up,
Our little cherished one;
'Twas hard to drink the bitter-cup,
And say, "Thy will be done."

And yet to cheer us in our woe
This precious thought is given, —
We have one darling still below,
But one is safe in heaven.

PATRIOTIC POEMS.

RALLYING SONG.

Come, rally around the old standard!

  Let our banner float out on the breeze!

For, thanks be to God and our pilot,

  The ship still outrides the rough seas.

Though the wind whistles shrill though her cord-

    age,

  And the sails in the tempest may rip,

We've faith in the skill of the helmsman

  Who stands at the wheel of the ship.

We know that his faith is the surest;

  We know that his courage is tried,

And his honor was ever the purest :

What more could we ask of our guide ?

When the storm gathered darkest and nearest,

No faltering fell from his lips :

Then a cheer for old " Abram," the pilot

Who stands at the helm of our ship.

The storm mutters yet to the southward,

And the sky is o'erclouded with gloom ;

For Heaven's sake, no half-hearted pilot,

Who will let us drift on to our doom !

The breakers still yawn to ingulf us :

If the bark from her anchorage slip,

Then give up the helm to old " Abram ; "

We know that his heart's in the ship.

Our enemies hate him and fear him :

Their hope even now groweth dim,

And they cry out, in hopeless despairing,
  "Give us any, ay, any but him!"
He has borne up our flag in disaster,
  And when victory perched on its tip;
Then give up the helm to old "Abram,"
  Who knows all the ropes of the ship.

He will carry our ship past the breakers;
  He will keep the flag free of all stain;
He has honored the trust that we gave him:
  We know we can trust him again.
Then rally once more round his standard,
  And let it ring loud from each lip,
"A cheer for our true-hearted pilot!
  We'll give him the helm of the ship."

A VOICE FROM "OUR BOYS."

We left our homes and hearthstones
    Three weary years ago :
'Neath the banner of our country
    We marched to meet the foe.
There were hearts that ached to breaking,
    And tears that fell like rain :
Do those heartaches count as nothing ?
    Were those tear-drops wept in vain ?

Mid dangers, toil, and perils
    Such as you may never know,
We have stood, a wall of valor,
    Twixt your hearthstones and the foe.

We have learned to smile at danger;
  We have learned to mock at pain:
But we ask you, O our brothers,
  Have we borne these things in vain?

We have borne our starry banner
  Over heaps of our own dead;
Where the shot rained thickest, fastest,
  We have followed if it led.
And, though battle-scarred and tattered,
  It has never known a stain:
Will ye dare to tell us, brothers,
  We have kept it pure in vain?

By the victories we have won you,
  By the laurels we have earned,
By the homes we've left behind us,
  By the comforts we have spurned,

By the bones that bleach unnumbered
On each trampled battle-plain,
We plead with you, our brothers,
Let us suffer not in vain !

By our marches and our battles,
By the blood that we have shed,
By the prisons where we languished,
By the memory of our dead,
By the hardships we have suffered,—
Fiercest hunger, thirst, and pain,—
We ask you, men and brothers,
Is our sacrifice in vain ?

Hark ! Vermont's snow-covered summits
Send a ringing sound of cheer,
And from Maine's dark, waving forests
Comes an echo loud and clear :

"Fear not, faint not! we are coming"

(So those joyful echoes say)

"To the music of the Union:

Abram leads us!—clear the way!"

GOD BLESS OUR SOLDIER BOYS.

THE fields are white and spotless; the chill
    north-wester blows;
The winter skies hang heavy beneath their
    weight of snow.
We sit beside the casement and watch the
    gathering storm,
And wonder if our soldiers in their canvas
    tents are warm;
And, when at eve we gather around the hearth-
    stone bright,
Each heart sends up a prayer, "God keep our
    soldier boys to-night!"

They left us in the spring time and in the
summer's glow;

All through the lonely autumn we saw our
loved ones go.

From all our noisy workshops, from every
bustling street,

We miss the kindly faces that we were wont
to meet;

They've gone to blot out treason, — to battle
for the right:

We send them with our blessing, — God bless
our boys to-night!

Some led the charge at Newbern, when the
rebel columns broke;

Some at Ball's Bluff fought nobly, and some
at Roanoke;

Some to New Orleans followed the flag of
stripes and stars;
Some won a Southern prison, and some immortal scars.
They have proved themselves true heroes in
many a bloody fight;
Oft tried, but ne'er found wanting, — God bless
them all to-night!

There's grief in every household; our land with
blood is red;
There's waiting for the absent, and weeping for
the dead.
We mourn our fallen heroes, but the living
claim our care;
We bless them at our firesides; we name them
in our prayer;

God guide them through all danger! God keep

them in the fight!

Where'er they light their camp-fires, God bless

our boys to-night!

THE COMING OF FREEDOM.

Long time the world in darkness lay

Beneath Oppression's iron sway;

And, e'en where Freedom once abode,

Her altar-fire but dimly glowed.

Earth waited long, with listening ear,

When sudden, like a thunder-stroke,

A deep voice through the silence broke,

 "Make way for Freedom!"

Make way for Freedom! for she comes

With flying flags and beating drums,

And her old keepers seek in vain

To weld anew her broken chain.

She holds no parley with her foes,

But right and left deals sturdy blows,

And vindicates her ancient fame

Mid cannons' roar and blood and flame:

    Make way for Freedom!

She stoops not now to plead her cause

Through the weak voice of trampled laws;

Lo, in the Ethiop's dusky hand

She lays her keen and flashing brand,

Points where her starry banners wave,

And bids him be no more a slave;

And, as her hosts go sweeping by,

His voice takes up their battle-cry,

    "Make way for Freedom!"

Oh, say not that our toil is vain!

We build anew fair Freedom's fame;

We lay the corner stone with tears;

But, gazing far down future years,

We see the finished temple stand

Towering to heaven, complete and grand,

And through its wide and ample door

The nations thronging evermore

    To worship Freedom.

Then who would weakly hesitate?

The passing hours are big with fate.

Will not each patriot heart reply,

"It is thy voice! Lord, here am I."

My country, thine shall be my fate;

My all to thee I consecrate;

Gladly I draw the sword for thee,

And fight, bleed, die, if need there be,

    "For thee and Freedom."

OUR FLAG.

I'LL sing my country's glorious flag,
  The proud old flag of yore,
That in the days long since gone by
  Our patriot fathers bore.
The dear old flag, long may it wave!
  'Twas bought with blood and scars, —
The legacy our fathers gave:
  God bless the stripes and stars!

What though, obscured in treason's night,
  Some stars have dimmed their rays,
And, wandering like a meteor's light,
  Shot madly from their place?

What though above the fertile fields,   •

    'Neath our old ensign won,

The broad "Palmetto" flaunts the breeze,

    Beneath a Southern sun?

Not ours the hand that drew the sword

    The first red drops that shed;

The guilt, the damning guilt of blood

    Be on our brother's head;

But war's red flag at length unfurled,

    We who have borne so long

Will teach our brethren and the world

    That patient hearts are strong.

Not ours the hand that snapped the chain,

    And drew its limbs asunder:

We strove to stay the storm in vain

    When first we heard its thunder,—

And history all time shall tell
  How long they spurned our prayers, —
That we might still be friends, and dwell
  In peace with them and theirs.

We've risen in our might at length :
  Our country's foe shall feel
An outraged nation's giant strength, —
  The strength of Northern steel.
No more we seek to mend the chain ;
  No more we woo with prayers :
Our cannon on the battle-plain
  Shall thunder back to theirs.

The Old Bay State has risen in might :
  Her arm is bared once more ;
Her war-cry ringing through the fight,
  " Remember Baltimore !"

No time for weak or coward words,
  No time for idle breath :
The man that draws a traitor's sword
  Shall meet a traitor's death.

"Our flag," thou hope of every land,
  Thou pride of every sea,
Our wealth, our strength, our heart's last blood,
  Shall all be given to thee.
Undimmed, unconquered, thou shalt wave
  In the red light of Mars,
Till the last freeman finds a grave
  Beneath the stripes and stars.

KISS ME, MOTHER, AND LET ME GO

Have you heard the news that I heard to-day, —
  The news that trembles on every lip?
The sky is darker again, they say,
  And breakers threaten the good old ship.
Our country calls on her sons again
  To strike in her name at a dastard foe:
She asks for six hundred thousand men;
  And I would be one, mother: let me go.

The love of country was born with me:
  I remember how my young heart would thrill
When I used to sit on my grandame's knee,
  And list to the story of Bunker Hill.

Life gushed out there in a rich red flood:
My grandsire fell in that fight, you know.
Would you have me shame the brave old blood?
Nay, kiss me, mother, and let me go.

Our flag, the flag of our hope and pride,
With its stars and stripes and its field of blue,
Is mocked, insulted, torn down, defiled,
And trampled upon by the rebel crew;
And England and France look on and sneer,
"Ha! queen of the earth thou art fallen low!"
Earth's down-trodden millions weep and fear:
So kiss me, mother, and let me go.

Under the burning Southern skies
Our brothers languish in heart-sick pain;
They turn to us with their pleading eyes:
O mother! say, shall they turn in vain?

Their ranks are thinning from sun to sun,

  Yet bravely they hold at bay the foe:

Shall we let them die there one by one?

  Nay, kiss me, mother, and let me go.

Can you selfishly cling to your household joys,

  Refusing the smallest tithe to yield,

While thousands of mothers are sending boys

  Beloved as yours to the battle-field?

Can you see my country call in vain,

  And restrain my arm from the needful blow?

Not so; though your heart should break with

    pain,

  You will kiss me, bless me, and bid me go.

FIGHT FOR THE FLAG.

Fight for the flag menaced now with pollu-
    tion ;
Fight for the freedom of country and State ;
Strike for the rights that the old Constitution
    Gave to the meanest as well as the great ;
Kneel while our banner floats out in its beauty ;
    Swear to defend it to life's latest breath,
Then to the field of your honor and duty
    March with the battle-cry, " Freedom or
    Death !"

A BALLAD OF THE WAR.

"My arm?" I lost it at Cedar Mountain.
 Ah, little one! that was a dreadful fight;
For brave blood flowed like a summer fountain,
 And the cannon roared till the fall of night.
Nay, nay! your question has done no harm,
    dear,
 Though it woke for a moment a thrill of pain;
For, whenever I look at my stump of an arm
    here,
 I seem to be living that day again.

A cloud of sulphurous haze hung o'er us
 As prone we lay in the trampled mire;

Shells burst above us, and right before us
  A rebel battery belched forth fire.
All at once to the front our colonel galloped,
  His form through the smoke looking dim and
      large :
" You see that battery, boys ! " he shouted :
  " We're ordered to take it.   Ready ! charge ! "

What a thrill I felt as the word was given !
  At once to his feet each soldier leapt ;
One long, wild shout went up to heaven,
  Then down on the foe like the wind we
      swept.
Each fought that day for his country's honor :
  We gained the edge of a slippery bank ;
I drove from his post a rebel gunner,
  And then — The rest is a perfect blank.

What need to tell of the days that followed,
  Each dragging painfully, slowly by,
Till, wearied out by my constant pleading,
  They sent me home, as they thought, to die?
My sire was dead, and my own loved mother
  Was wasting away with toil and care;
I'd a little sister and feeble brother;
  And I — I could be but a burden there.

And so this peddler's trunk I bought me;
  Filled it with needles, pins, tape, and thread,
Housewife's stores, as my mother taught me,
  And I sell them to win my daily bread.
When the frost on the fields lies still and hoary,
  My way through the village streets I take;
My empty coat-sleeve tells its story,
  And they're kind to me for the old flag's
    sake.

It was not regret that made me falter,

  Nor sorrow that made my eye grow dim :

I offered all on my country's altar,

  And she was pleased to accept a limb.

Maimed, but yet to regrets a stranger,

  The thought that gives me the keenest pain

Is this, — were my country once more in danger,

  I never could fight in her ranks again.

BE TRUE TO THE FLAG OF THE UNION.

[JULY 22, 1861.]

Not with bright garlands of the graceful bay

We twine to-day our banner's drooping folds,

But wreathed with sable hanging like a pall

Over its field of blue, and shutting out

Its stars, even as from so many homes

Hope's star to-day has faded ; let us go

To hang the cypress o'er our warriors' tombs :

Ah me ! methinks 'twas only yesterday

That all the calm, blue air was rent with
    cheers,

And drums beat, banners waved, and music
        played,
As they, our gallant and true-hearted ones,
Went from us, bearing forth our country's flag,
To battle in our country's holy cause.
We looked upon them, brave and beautiful,
And all our hearts were stirred with love and
        pride.
"Go forth," we said, "O brothers dear! up-
        hold
The flag we love and honor! Heaven will smile
Upon you; God will give you victory;
And we, — whom force of circumstance compels
To stay behind you, — doubt not that our
        hearts
Go forward with you; doubt not, brothers,
        friends,
That you shall be remembered.

From the shores
Of Maine to California anxious eyes
Are turned on you; and knees that never bent,
And lips that never opened yet to crave
Heaven's blessings on themselves, with daily
prayers
Besiege the throne of God in your behalf.
Go forth, O brothers! for ye cannot fail."

And so they left us. Thus we sent them forth
To shame, defeat, and death. Oh, we must
weep,
E'en though the victors gloat upon our tears!
For Nature will o'erleap the narrow bounds
That Pride would set her, and assert herself
In grief that will have way; yet let them pause.
Let them not glory in our grief too much:
It bodes them little good. Appalled and stunned,

Borne down by crushing sorrow for our dead

Who lie unburied on Potomac's shore,

We may be now; but, when we strike again,

Let them beware! From every crimson drop

That yesterday our loved ones shed like rain

Goes up a cry for vengeance, and the eyes

That yet are red with weeping have a flash

As terrible as lightning.

      Farewell, tears!

Vain sorrow will not bring them back to us:

Be it ours, then, to avenge them!

BE FIRM IN BATTLE FOR THE UNION.

Brothers, take this holy flag!
  We can trust it in your keeping;
Guard it ever with your lives,
  Cherish it **with love** unsleeping;
And, if only one should come
  Back to tell the bloody story,
Let him bring that banner **home**
  Gleaming with its ancient glory.

Side by side upon the field
  They have waved in many **a** battle:
Bear **it** on the battle-field
  Mid the wounded and the dying;

Make your strong right arms its shield;
Ever follow where 'tis flying.
From their homes in yonder sky
Freedom's sires are watching o'er you:
Be their names your battle-cry
As you drive the foe before you.

Never trail it in defeat,
Lest the world should prove a scorner:
Life can never more be sweet
That is purchased by dishonor.
When you stand before the foe,
Face to face in line of battle,
E'er the first red blood-drop flow, .
Or begins the cannon's rattle,
Think how we are praying for you;
Know that every lip would say,
Die, but suffer not dishonor.

THE MIDNIGHT BIVOUAC.

The winter stars shine cold on high;
  The hoar-frost glitters on the ground;
The camp-fires burn with smouldering light;
  My comrades sleep around.

A full moon hangs above the land,
  And bare and black against the sky
The blasted cedars stand.

  A hurried footstep drawing near:
I hear his rifle click, and then
  His challenge rings out clear, —

"Halt! who comes there?" — "A friend." — "Pass
  Three steps, and give the countersign!"

"Right! Pass on, friend." A quick, firm tread
    Goes ringing down the line.
Sleep on, tired brothers! take your rest,
    For night is wearing fast away;
The moon is sinking in the west;
    The morn may bring the fray.

THE CAPTAIN'S LETTER.[1]

IN MEMORIAM.

I AM writing to you, lady, with an aching heart
  and brain,
Knowing well that every sentence will give you
  bitter pain ;
Will dim the light within your eyes, and cloud
  your brow with gloom,
And bring dark clouds of sorrow to your far-off
  peaceful home.

[1] Written by N. A. W. Priest after reading Capt. Buffum's letter to me after the death of my husband, G. C. Parker, November, 1862. — CARRIE L. R. PARKER.

Knowing well the fearful anguish that will wring your spirit's core

When you tell your little daughters that their father is no more;

Full well, believe me, lady, do his mourning comrades know,

By the sadness they experience, what must be your bitter woe.

I was his captain, lady! 'Neath the soldier's blouse of blue

Never lived a nobler spirit, never throbbed a heart more true;

Ever cheerful mid privations, since his soldier life began;

When the bugle called to duty, he was ever in the van;

Loving freedom, hating slavery as a wrong of
  God accursed :
Death passed by meaner spirits, and took the
  noblest first.
True, he fell not in the battle ; but no less his
  name shall stand
In the glorious list of martyrs who have died
  to save their land.

We laid him down to slumber in a deep, unbroken rest,
Far from his native valleys, and the hearts that
  loved him best ;
We placed a simple headboard to mark the hal-
  lowed spot,
And left him there with feelings that will never
  be forgot ;

We buried him at twilight when the sun had
    sunk to rest
In his crimson-curtained chamber in the brightly
    glowing west;
And, gliding with slow footsteps o'er the east-
    ern hills afar,
Evening donned her cool, gray mantle, and
    pinned it with a star.

Rough was the narrow coffin that his fellow-
    soldiers bore,
And we laid him gently in it in the uniform he
    wore;
The chaplain made a prayer; brief and solemn
    words were said,
And we fired a parting volley o'er the poor,
    unconscious head.

There was little time for mourning, and none
    for idle show:
Long our march had been and **weary**; we had
    farther yet to go.
We heard the bugle calling as beside his grave
    we wept,
And we bivouacked at midnight miles away
    from where he slept.

Your grief is shared by thousands over all our
    bleeding land;
By desolated hearthstones weeping wives and
    children stand,
And gray-haired parents mourn and watch and
    wait in speechless pain
For tidings from the loved ones who will never
    come again.

Farewell, farewell, dear lady! I know how poor and weak
Would be any words of comfort that I might try to speak.
God's ways are dark and fearful, but he judgeth for the best :
May he take you in his keeping, and give you peace and rest !

CARRIE.

I was sitting and thinking to-night, Cal,
  Of days that have passed away :
They passed on the rapid wing of time,
  And we could not make them stay ;
They were bright and beautiful days, Cal,
  And sorrow was but a name :
It passed, and the sky was blue and fair
  As it was before it came.

I was sitting and thinking to-night, Cal,
  Of the castles we built in air :
They were all realites then, Cal,
  But frail although they were fair ;

And one by one they fall, Cal,

    Before the truths of life,

And our girlhood's golden dreams, Cal,

    Are lost in care and strife.

Oh ! life is a weary way, Cal,

    Illumed by a flickering light ;

And well for us if it be not lost,

    And we left in shades of night.

Now do not take this as a " poem," Cal:

    'Tis only an idle scrawl ;

I had but a minute before it was penned, —

    No thought of writing at all.

A DREAM OF THE BRAVE.

"I had a dream that was not all a dream."

Last night, when the moon was setting,
  And the day's last beam had flown,
Oppressed with a nameless sadness,
  I wandered out alone;
I sat me down to ponder
  On the trunk of a fallen tree,
And I saw a vision that haunts me still:
  List! and I will tell it thee.

Methought I stood near a forest,
  Where I never had been before;

I could see a winding river

  Lapping a broad, green shore.

Many a sail was gliding

  Silently down the stream ;

And dotting the hills and valleys,

  I could see the white tents gleam.

Then out of the gloomy forest,

  Where I silently stood apart,

Came strains of solemn music

  That thrilled to my very heart.

Sad and dirge-like and mournful,

  It swelled to the summer skies,

And touched a fountain of tear-drops

  That welled up into my eyes.

Nearer it came, and nearer ;

  And methought I turned my head,

And saw a band of soldiers
  Bringing **a brother** dead.
Steadily moved they onward
  Through the forest's checkered **shade**;
And still I watched their coming,
  And the solemn music **played**.

They passed me, but **still I** lingered;
  They climbed to the hill-top's crown,
And **then** at their leader's signal
  They laid their dead comrade down.
And there by the **winding river,**
  Close to its shining wave,
They broke the green turf of summer,
  And hollowed a narrow grave.

They were bearded, **rough, and** sunburnt,
  And their **eyes** looked fierce and wild;

But they lifted the dead one gently,

   As a mother might lift her child.

They could not give him a coffin ;

   But they smoothed his narrow bed,

And planted our starry banner

   Over his slumbering head.

No fond sister or mother

   Pressed for the parting look ;

No kind father or brother

   In the solemn rite partook.

Only those few tried comrades

   Stood with uncovered head,

And the tears from their rough cheeks

   Dropped on the quiet dead ;

Dropped on the curls of auburn ;

   Dropped on the close-shut eyes,

And the face in its boyish beauty
  Upturned to the mocking skies.
The notes of a distant bugle
  Came faint on the passing air:
So they gave him a parting volley,
  And left him to slumber there.

You smile, but your eyes are filling:
  "It was only a dream," you say.
Ah! but the thing I dreamed of
  Is happening every day.
In swamp and forest and valley,
  And down by the river's waves,
Even now, while you sit there smiling,
  They are making our soldiers' graves.

MOONLIGHT.

I HATE the beautiful moonlight
   That is falling so white and still
On the dim and shadowy forest,
   And the brown and barren hill.
It haunts me with vague misgivings,
   And restless, unquiet fears,
And fills my heart with a sadness
   That lieth too deep for tears.

For I think of a far-off camp-ground
   That is bathed in this soft, rich light;
I can see the moon's rays gleaming
   On the tents of snowy white;

But all is still and peaceful
  As a city of the dead,
Save when the hush is broken
  By the sentinels' measured tread.

I busy my mind by daylight
  In a thousand useless ways ;
I smile at my children's prattle,
  Or join in their merry plays ;
But, when the shadows of evening
  Gather around my home,
I find myself listening, waiting,
  For a step that will not come.

I light my lamp in the evening,
  And sit by the children's bed,
While, with soft palms pressed together,
  The childish prayer is said.

But my heart sinks cold within me,
  And the tear-drop dims my sight,
When my little Lizzie asks me,
  "Will my father come to-night?"

"Nay, not to-night, my darling,"
  My tremulous voice replies;
And a transient shadow hovers
  In the depth of her violet eyes.
To her 'tis an oft-told answer,
  Forgotten as soon as heard;
But my little womanly Alice
  Will never forget a word.

God knows I would not recall him,
  No, not if my heart should break:
I have given him to his country
  For our perilled freedom's sake.

But, alas! for the homes made lonely,
And the hearts left desolate!
God pity us helpless women,
Who can only weep and wait!

THE BALL AT THE WHITE HOUSE.

The White House is radiant with beauty and
    light ;
The "heads of the nation" are merry to-night ;
And fair cheeks are blooming, and dark eyes
    grow bright,
  Responsive to passionate glances.
Not a lip breathes a sigh ; not a brow speaks of
    care :
The surgeon and nurse take their long, weary
    rounds,
And brave hearts bleed slowly away through
    great wounds,
  That would frighten each delicate dancer.

How delicious the wine that you daintily sip
Would taste to the parched tongue and feverish
    lip !
Though 'twere only a drop, just to moisten the
    tip,
  Bah ! nonsense ! sour gruel will answer.

To-night, with the damp, frosty earth for a bed,
And stars shining through the torn tent over-
    head,
Full many a soldier has laid down his head,
  And sighed for the blanket he needed.
Do they murmur ? then punish the base, thank-
    less churls.
"It is fitting" that you should wear "satins"
    and pearls,
And twine costly flowers in your beautiful curls,
  And "fit" that *they* suffer unheeded.

Hunted like tigers in mountain and glen,

Forced to find refuge in forest and den,

It would be a rare picture no doubt to these

men,

  The sight of your splendor and beauty.

Flowers breathe out their life on this festival

night,

To sweeten the air and gladden the sight;

Silks rustle, and diamonds flash in the light,

  And the music grows thrilling and tender.

Who would hint in the midst of their gay, joy-

ous life

Of a treasury empty, and brothers at strife?

Who would guess that the nation is struggling

for life

  In the midst of such feasting and splendor?

To-night, with a heart rent with anguish and

   care,

The poor, - hunted " Unionist " creeps from his

   lair,

And looks up to heaven with a half-uttered

   prayer,

   But dreams not of shrinking from duty.

The old ship of state is the sport of the sea :

Her moorings are gone, breakers roar on her

   lee,

   And rougher each hour grows the weather.

Bid your music swell loud; let the dance still

   go on ;

And when the crash comes, and the last plank

   is gone,

   We will go to the bottom together.

MASSACHUSETTS TO CALIFORNIA.

Fair dweller on a distant strand
    The same blue waves are beating,
Across broad leagues of sea and land
    The Bay State sends you greeting !
We stretch toward you an honest hand ;
    We glory in your beauty :
Dear younger sister of our band,
    Accept a sister's duty.

Unchanged and peaceful flows your life,
    Unmoved by our disorders ;
The din of this tremendous strife,
    Scarce reaches to your borders.

In peaceful fields your farmers reap,

  And plenty fills their measures;

Your miners pierce the mountains steep,

  And bring out golden treasures.

Our homes are sad and desolate,

  Our hearthstones dark and lonely;

Still every pulse beats fondly yet

  For the good Union only.

We send our best and bravest forth

  Unshrinking to the slaughter;

We lavish gold in sums untold;

  We pour our blood like water.

We send no cowards to the field

  To shame our ancient glory;

Our sons will sooner die than yield, —

  Let Ball's Bluff tell the story.

You sit beneath the same broad flag:

  Ties, strong and powerful, bind us;

We march to meet the battle's heat, —

  Fall in, fall in behind us.

Fair dweller on a distant strand

  The same broad sea is beating,

Across wide leagues of wave and land

  The Bay State sends you greeting!

Arise! stretch forth your helping hand

  To save the land we cherish!

Shoulder to shoulder we must stand,

  Or side by side we perish.

LEVEE.

WRITTEN TO BE SUNG AT THE FIREMEN'S ANNIVERSARY

FEBRUARY, 1863.

A BAND of friends and brothers dear,
  We gather here to-night ;
And every lip is wreathed in smiles,
  And every eye is bright.
We meet in peace and friendship,
  Secure from all alarm :
Then honor to the gallant men
  Who guard our homes from harm !

CHORUS.

Hurrah, for our brave firemen !
  Swell the chorus louder, higher :

All honor to the gallant men
   Who guard our homes from fire!

They make no weeping orphans;
   They fill no yawning grave;
Theirs is a noble mission, for
   They conquer but to save.
We fear not when the hungry flames
   Come creeping nigh and nigher,
For they've won full many a triumph
   O'er the demon King of Fire.

CHORUS.

Hurrah for our brave firemen!
   Swell the chorus louder, higher:
They've won full many a triumph
   O'er the demon King of Fire.

We meet to-night, as we have met
  For many a rolling year;
But manly forms are absent now
  That used to meet us here.
They heard our country calling,
  And their hearts were strong and true;
So they dropped the fireman's scarlet coat
  For the soldier's blouse of blue.

CHORUS.

Hurrah for our brave brothers,
  Whose hearts were strong and true,
Who dropped the fireman's jacket
  For the soldier's blouse of blue!

They sit long weary miles away
  Around the camp-fire's light;

And yet we seem to hear them say,

　"Remember us to-night.

We've parents, homes, and loved ones,

　We left at duty's call;

You gave of your abundance,

　But we have given all."

CHORUS.

Hurrah for our brave brothers!

　They sprang at duty's call:

We come to-night to give our mite

　To those who've given their all.

March on! march on to victory,

　O brothers brave and true!

Be sure the hearts that stay behind

　Are beating warm for you.

Our eager eyes will watch you :

We shall cherish every name ;

We sorrow in your sorrows ;

We shall glory in your fame.

CHORUS.

Have courage, faith, and patience,

For your cause is just and right :

God grant that you may meet us here

A twelve-month from to-night !

EXPOSURE TO A "DRAFT."

Of the danger from "exposure to a draft," we
often read

That it generates disorders which are very bad
indeed ;

But the danger from "exposure to a draft" was
ne'er so great

As, I judge from indications, it has grown to
be of late.

Of all our loyal citizens, I think I cannot tell

Of more than half a dozen who are "feeling
very well ; "

And so various are the phases of the illness from one cause,

That I wonder if Dame Nature still is steadfast to her laws.

One is halt, one is blind, a third is deaf as any post;

A fourth gone in consumption,—can hardly walk at most;

A fifth is dying daily from a weakness of the spine,

And a sixth is fading slowly in a general decline.

There Jenkins, stalworth-looking, standing six feet in his shoes,

And his cheeks, so plump, look ruddy as the sunset crimson hues;

But alas! the fond delusion! 'tis a *hectic flush*
    we see;
'Tis a pulmonary **Jenkins**, who ere long must
    cease to be.

There is Muggins, with a form protrusive and
    rotund;
But the *dropsy*, — that deceitful, insidious com-
    plaint,
Is what has made him look so: you may ask
    him if it haint.

If Jeff Davis was a man of any gumption, he
    would know
That it's wasting **ammunition** to shoot a dying
    foe :

Just let him halt in Dixie till a few more
  months have sped,
And I think our loyal citizens will nearly all
  be dead.

WAR TO THE KNIFE.

"ONCE more to the combat with rekindled zeal,

Our flag to the breeze, and our hands to the

    steel."

Bare every true arm for the perilous fight,

Then strike, and strike boldly for God and the

    right !

No time to draw backward with faltering breath ;

We deal with a foe that is cruel as death ;

Let us grant no more parleys to treason and

    guilt ;

Give them "war to the knife, and the knife to

    the hilt."

They have broken their oath without shadow of

cause ;

They have trampled our banners, and mocked

at our laws ;

In the blood of our brothers their hands have

grown red ;

They have murdered our wounded and mangled

. our dead.

Is this, then, the time to grow pale, and cry,

" Peace ! "

Shall we throw down our weapons to dastards

like these ?

No ! on, to avenge the brave blood they have spilt !

Give them "war to the knife, and the knife to

the hilt."

For we're sworn by an oath that we will not recall,

For our country to conquer, or gloriously fall ;

Ne'er to lay down our arms, unless in death's
    rest,
Till our country again is united and blest.
Already, beside the Potomac's blue flood,
Our brothers by hundreds have sealed it with
    blood ;
Their mission is ended, their task nobly done,
They have left us to finish the work they be-
    gun.

"Once more to the combat!" we brook no de-
    lay :
Let them boast of their triumph, and taunt
    while they may ;
Loud cannon and steel shall bear back our
    reply,
"We will wipe the foul stain from our banners,
    or die."

On, brothers! we fight in humanity's cause

For the country we love, and her glorious laws,

For the temple of freedom our forefathers built:

Give them "war to the knife, and the knife to

the hilt."

OUR VICTORY.

Ring out to-night, O sweet-voiced bells,
Your maddest, merriest peal !
Deep-throated cannon, speak and tell
The gushing joy we feel !
Huzza ! huzza ! the day is won !
Light every hill with fires,
And let the electric tidings run
Along a thousand wires.

We gaze upon our flag to-night
Without a sense of pain ;
It comes victorious from the fight,
Untarnished by a stain.

Trampled in dust by traitors' feet
  Those starry folds have been;
But our just vengeance is complete;
  This day has washed it clean.

We hoped for this; for this we prayed
  Through many a gloomy day;
And sometimes hope would almost fade
  Before the long delay.
We longed to hear the clash of steel
  Along our border line,
And see the cause of treason reel
  And totter in decline.

And yet the cup has its alloy;
  Full many a cheek is pale,
And mixed with every burst of joy
  Goes up a deep, sad wail,

We read the proud and joyful news
    With pangs of heartfelt pain,
And smiles and tear-drops interfuse
    Like April sun and rain.

Alas for those who wear the crown
    Of thorns that is not mine,
Who laid their heart's best jewel down
    Upon their country's shrine!
God pity those who hear the bells,
    And shudder all the while,
Who, while's joy's tide around them swells,
    Can feel no heart to smile!

We hear the shouts of victory;
    Hope sings and soars anew,
And then we turn, O hearts bereaved,
    To weep and pray for you!

Sweet Christ, drop thy divinest balm
Into the hearts that grieve,
And make them feel that blessed calm
Which only thou canst give!

LAUS DEO.

Sing to the Lord our helper! He hath been our
    strength and might;
He hath girded on His armor: our foes are put
    to flight;
In every sore disaster He has been our guide
    and friend.
Long the way has been, and fearful; but our
    eyes can see the end:
'Twere worth ten lives, though every life could
    count a hundred years,
But to have been in Richmond to have heard
    our soldiers' cheers,

And **the bands of** music playing, and the deep-
mouth cannon's **roar,**

When the old "star-spangled banner" **rose** on
Richmond's walls once more,

Where so long Rebellion's emblem has been dar-
ingly **unfurled,**

A menace to our country, and an **insult to** the
world !

Tremble, O deserted city! where the walls of
Libby **stand,**

A terror and a loathing to a desolated land.

Didst thou think the captive's tear-drop, and **his**
bitter, **bitter** moan,

Were not borne by pitying angels straight before
the great white throne?

Didst thou think God's ear was deafened? didst
thou think He could not hear?

Didst thou think His arm was shortened, that
　　He could not punish thee?
Lo, thy day of reckoning cometh! low is thy
　　proud, rebellious head;
Thou shalt drink thy tears like water; thou shalt
　　eat sin's bitter bread:
There shall be not one to pity when thy woe
　　for pity calls.
Tremble! tremble, wicked city! for God's hand
　　in justice falls.

Glory, glory! morning cometh!　Long and dark
　　has been the night,
And our eyes have ached with weeping and with
　　watching for the light.
Long we lavished gold uncounted, long we poured
　　our blood like rain,

And we rallied to the conflict bravely, sternly,
but in vain;
For God priced our freedom higher, and His
voice at first heard low,
Kept ringing louder, clearer, "Let my captive
people go.
While they toil and weep in bondage, all your
valor shall be vain;
Dare not hope that **I will bless** you while you
bind one sufferer's chain."
And at last, in mute obedience, we listened to
the call,
And, look! the dear old banner **waves on Richmond's** conquered wall.

Glory, glory! **Ransomed nation, lift** one long,
exultant shout:

Let the hill-tops blaze with bonfires; fling the
     flag we've fought for out;
Ring, O tuneful bells of freedom, till the very
     steeple reel,
For the armèd head of treason lies 'neath Lib-
     erty's mailed heel!
Speak with tongues of flame, O cannon! send
     thy joyful tidings round;
Roar till the far skies re-echo, and the whole
     world hears the sound,
And tell earth's quaking despots, as they list
     with straining ears,
"Lo, the great Republic liveth;" thus she an-
     swers to your queries;
Thus to your very strongholds is her proud
     defiance hurled.
Glory! God is throned in heaven, and there's
     freedom for the world.

HYMN.

ON THE DEATH OF PRESIDENT LINCOLN,

APRIL 19, 1865.

O GOD forever nigh,
Who hear'st Thy people's cry,
Incline Thine ear!
We mourn our noble dead,
Our nation's honored head:
Come, and Thy influence shed,
Our hearts to cheer.

Through these long, weary years
Of darkness, doubts, and fears,
He led our way:

He taught us faith and hope;
He shared our bitter cup;
He bore our banner up
   In danger's day.

Now, when the sky grows bright
With victory, — glorious light, —·
   The nation weeps.
Ah! dreadful was the blow
That laid our leader low;
But while we bow in woe
   He calmly sleeps.

Rest calmly, sainted dust:
We will fulfil the trust
   Imposed by thee.

The land that holds thy grave,

The land thou diedst to save,

Shall never own a slave :

All shall be free.

POEMS OF NATURE.

INVOCATION.

I'M tired of strife; I'm sick of heartless living:
    Fain would I from the world's rude jostling
        flee.
No longer toward youth's high ideal striving,
    Thy child, O mother Nature! turns to thee.

For thou canst comfort when the heart is sorest;
    Oh, let me take thy hand and walk with thee,
And watch thee sowing acorns in the forest,
    Or scattering spring's blue violets o'er the lea.

Let me sit with thee 'neath the maples' shadows,
    Or watch upon the hills to see thee pass;

Teach me to trace thy footsteps in the meadows
  By the bright cowslips dotting all the grass.

Speak to me in the murmur of the river;
  Sing to me with thy thousand voices sweet;
Hold my tired head, and let me sit forever
  Drinking in rest and patience at thy feet.

So shall I rise above earth's selfish sorrow;
  So shall I win new strength to bear life's
    pain;
And, waiting hopefully for "heaven to-morrow,"
  Take up my burden, and press on again.

NATURE.

I worship Nature in her mildest mood,
In the dark mountain or the silent wood;
I love the quiet of her summer hours,
Her singing birds and many-colored flowers;
Not less I love her when, arrayed in white,
The earth reflects the sun's unclouded light.
Oh! Nature's hand is bountiful and kind:
She is a foster-mother to the mind.
Not with harsh words she leads the erring
To Virtue's road from Misery's thorny track;
She speaks to him in tones as soft and mild
As the fond mother to an erring child;

She whispers him from sunny glen and wood,

From crowded street and dreary solitude;

She sends the sunshine and the gentle shower;

She smiles on him from every wayside flower;

And, when the daylight in the west grows dim,

She lights the evening's twinkling lamps for

    him,

Till he repent, by love and beauty won,

The wrong and evil he hath blindly done,

And wins his way with penitence and tears

Back to the purity of earlier years.

COMFORT IN NATURE.

THERE is a quiet spot — I know it well —
'Where the wild lily hangs its spotted bell;
And upward glancing through its **pale-green**
    leaves,
With **meck** eyes of tears like one that grieves,
The **violet** unfolds its leaves of blue
To catch the sunshine, and to drink the dew;
And, with a look half-timid and half-bold,
The cowslip rears its tiny cup of gold.
There **blooms the** daisy, fairest **child** of Spring,
And there the robin earliest comes to sing,
And breezes kiss the willows as they pass,
And crickets chirp and rustle in the grass,

And the gay brook in shade or sunshine ever
Goes singing on to join the restless river.

And sometimes when my heart is full of care,
Or bound with earthly chains, I wander there,
And, half reclining on the sunny grass,
I watch the flitting shadows come and pass,
And see the dazzling sunrays as they gleam
Upon the dimpling eddies of the stream ;
Or listen to the love-songs of the birds,
Sweeter than any ever set to words,
Till cares and trials fade, or only seem
Like the vague memory of some troubled dream,
Or some sad, thrilling music heard through
     tears
At first, but after lapse of many years
Thought of but seldom, or perchance forgot ;
And I rise up contented with my lot.

LIFE.

A SONNET.

The rain is falling, and the skies are gray;
    Dark, sullen clouds go flying back and forth ;
Yet I can see the golden sunshine play
    Upon yon mountain summit of the north.
And they who stand upon its topmost height
    Can bask them in the warm and cheering
        beam,
While underneath the skies look dark as night,
    And through·rent clouds the fiery lightnings
        gleam :
So we, tired travellers through a desert land,
    Beset on every side by doubts and strife,

Can at the best but dimly understand

What is 'the transient thing that men call life :

But, when from all earth's clogs our souls are free,

How wide, how grand, will our unbounded

prospect be !

FLOWERS.

Flowers! are they not the alphabet of angels,
　　Wherein they write God's pure and holy
　　　　will?
Are they not sent to us like sweet evangels
　　To teach us how he loves earth's children
　　　　still?

For, from the ever-blooming tropic's bowers
　　Unto the arctics, there is scarce a spot
That may not boast the precious boon of
　　　　flowers, —
　　That this sweet gift of God enlightens not.

Flowers! bring the fragrant, creamy orange-
    blossom
  To grace the white brow of the fair young
    bride;
Wreathe in her hair, and lay them on her bosom:
  By them her purity is typified.

Flowers for the festal board! bring summer
    roses,
  That shake such perfume from their hearts
    of gold,
And each gay flower that to the sun uncloses,
  And shuts again when night comes, dark. and
    cold.

Flowers for the dead! oh, bring the drooping lily;
  Bring snowy buds just bursting through their
    green,

To lay upon the form so pale and chilly, —

The casket where the precious gem has been.

Flowers for the young! oh, lead the feet of
childhood,

Ere yet they enter sin's bewildering mazes,

To every flower-loved haunt in vale or wildwood,

And through the meadow buttercups and
daisies.

Flowers! are they not the alphabet of angels,

Wherein their brightest, purest thoughts are
spelt?

Are they not sent to us as God's evangels,

Voiceless, yet speaking words that may be
felt?

SPRING MEMORIES.

The lilac-buds begin to swell;

The cowslip rears its yellow bell;

And deep in every sunny dell

  The wild arbutus-blossoms spring;

The maples show pale tufts of leaves;

And, from their nests beneath the eaves,

  The glancing swallows soar and sing.

The meadow's violets are blue;

The rosebuds have a carmine hue,

Like the warm flush that ripples through

  The whiteness of a maiden's cheeks;

And from the pine-grove on the hill
I hear the lonely whip-poor-will,
That I can almost fancy speaks.

In such bright spring-times long ago,
Before our hearts had learned to know
There are such words as care and woe
And weariness and pain and strife,
Beneath the dome of May's blue sky,
My dark-eyed sister Lu and I
Spent hours and days of childhood's life.

We plucked the violets white and blue ;
Our bare feet brushed morn's earliest dew
From paths where the wild strawberries grew ;
And well we knew each forest glade
Where the wild partridge reared her young,
And where the robins earliest sung,
And where the summer longest staid.

How blue the skies stretched overhead !
How gorgeous seemed the rose's red !
And the green carpet for us spread
Was wrought with richest flowers ; the sands,
With shining pebbles dotted o'er,
Seemed to us like the golden floor
That poets give to fairylands.

Oh that the May-time's balmy breath
Could bring back childhood's trust and faith,
That makes all things seem bright, and death
Seems only like a sweet repose,
From which with new and strengthened powers
We'd wake, as wake the April flowers
From underneath December's snows !

THE VOICE OF SPRING.

I am God's limner. When the sunshine round
    them
  First tempts the squirrel and the brown-
    winged bee
From their retreat, and, freed from ice that
    bound them,
  The mountain-rills leap downward to the
    sea,
With silent fingers through the sunny hours
  I dress the forest trees in robes of green,
And wake to life again the pale, sweet flowers
  That grace the fair of the May-day queen.

I tinge the violet's pensive eyes with azure;

I gild the buttercups with purest gold;

And, 'neath my smiles on the bleak Alpine

glacier,

The harebell nods unconscious of the cold.

Deep in the forest aisles of gloomy splendor

The starwort specks the moss-like flakes of

light,

And the wood-laurel hangs on branches slender

Its tiny honey-cups of pink and white.

Up through the fresh green grass that clothes

the meadow,

Like stars the yellow dandelions look;

And the forget-me-not blooms in the shadow

Of alders that o'erhang the meadow brook;

A thread of silver through its banks doth glisten;

And there at noon the cattle crowd to drink,

Or stand with half-shut eyes, and seem to listen
The tinkling music of the bobolink.

Earth, sea, and air beneath my presence
    lighten;
And even the skies a deeper azure catch;
And at the sunset hour they flush and brighten
    In pictures Claude and Raphael ne'er could
        match.
Painted upon the placid sky of even
    They look so beautiful, that, while they last,
One might half fancy it the gate of heaven,
    Through which some shining angel just had
        passed.

IMPATIENCE.

I am longing for the summer,
  For the long, glad summer days;
For the river's dreamy murmur,
  And the wild birds' gushing lays;
For the breath of countless flowers
  By the zephyr borne along:
Oh, the joyous summer hours!
  They can never seem too long.

Snow lies upon the meadow,
  Where the violet's azure cup,
From beneath the alder's shadow,
  In the spring-time peepeth up;

And the hill is shrouded over,

  Where in summer-time the breeze

Waved a rich sea of clover,

  Bright with butterflies and bees.

White the forest, in whose mazes

  I have wandered many a day,

And the valleys filled with daisies

  Where the drowsy cattle lay ;

And I long to hear the rustle

  Of the south wind through the leaves,

And to see the swallows nestle

  In their nests beneath the eaves.

Where the willows' golden tassels

  Touched the dimpling stream below ;

And, like fleets of fairy vessels,

  Swung white lilies to and fro,

Dark and sullen glides the river
'Neath its icy fetters fast;
And the leafless willows shiver
In the shrieking northern blast.

I am longing for the summer,
With its long, bright sunny days;
For the river's dreamy murmur,
And the song-bird's gushing lays:
I am weary of the winter,
With its long and dreary reign,
And I wait the joyous summer
With impatience that is pain.

WHIMS.

I love to sit in the twilight
  When the fire is old and dim,
And hear in the click of the embers
  A tale that is ghostly and grim ;

To trace in the feathery ashes
  The faces and forms of things
That come to my nightly vision,
  And stir up my soul with wings ;

To feel, as the shadows creep closer,
  A thrill in the trancèd air,

Like the breath of a brooding spirit,
   The wraith of a wrestling prayer.

When the heart of the midnight is beating
   Weird time with the watch on the wall,
And, pillowed on my heart, is dreaming
   The thought that is dearest of all, —

I love to lie low in the darkness,
   And hear the storm-spirits go by,
With a wrench at my window-shutter,
   And a wailing, piteous cry;

To gather still closer my thoughts so true
   In the face of the scurrying foe,
And go maundering down the river of sleep
   With all the sweet voices I know.

I love the thin cry of the cricket

On the hearth or the lonely moor;

The woodpecker rat-a-tat tapping,

Like Death, at the oldest door.

There is a spell in the knell of the faded leaf;

And, of all the days in the year,

I love the red, ripe carnival time

Old Autumn makes over his bier.

THE WINTER RAIN.

The winter rain, the winter rain,
  I love to see it fall
Upon the white and stainless snow
  Or the half-covered wall.
Pray tell me why a winter rain
  Is pleasanter to see
Than falling drops of other rain:
  I'm sure it is to me.

I know not why the tinkling sound
  Of falling raindrops well
Should o'er my heart and in my mind
  Exert a witching spell;

Yet, in whate'er the spell exists,
  It is a joy to me,
And I would not dissolve the charm
  For hours of merry glee.

The dark, the thick, the spreading cloud,
  From which the raindrops come,
Is brighter to my eyes than all
  The pure cerulean dome.
It may be that it seems like spring
  To see the falling rain,
As if the leaves and buds would grow,
  And blossoms come again;

That birds again will greet the air
  With their rich notes of love,
And warmer subeams gild with light
  The azure skies above.

There is a pensive quietness
    In that soft, dropping sound,
That fills my heart with happiness,
    Though all be dark around.

And so where'er my lot is cast,
    On valley, hill, or plain,
This sound will please while life shall last, —
    The dropping of the rain.

A GLIMPSE FROM MY WINDOW.

'Tis evening! the stars in their beauty are
   shining,
  And brightly they beam on this fair earth of
   ours ;
And gentle and noiseless the dewdrops are falling
  On earth's verdant bosom and beautiful flowers.

The song of the birds through the still air is
   stealing,
  And the cricket's shrill note on the zephyr is
   borne ;

And gushings of music, now joyfully pealing,
    With hum of the forest, and rustling of corn.

Such nights and such beauty were not made
    for sleeping,
    But given to cheer us in life's stormy way,
To cheer our path onward, and guide our steps
    upward
    To regions of perfect, unchangeable day.

FLOATING DOWN THE RIVER.

Sunset fades behind the hill,
  Twilight drops her spangled veil,
And the love-born whip-poor-will,
  Tells his woe **to** every **gale.**
Stars gleam tremblingly from the **sky**;
  On the stream the moonbeams **quiver**;
And our boat goes silently
  Floating, floating down **the river.**

Waves flash backward from the oar;
  Then break rippling on the strand;
Fireflies light the lamps on the shore;
  Earth seems some enchanted land:

To the south wind's balmy sigh
  Willows bend and aspens shiver,
And our boat goes silently
  Floating, floating down the river.

There the rude bridge spans the stream;
  Deep and dark the waters lie,
Still as Lethe's fabled dream,
  Black as midnight's noonless sky;
And the night-bird's sudden cry
  Makes the startling dreamer shiver,
While the boat goes silently
  Floating, floating down the river.

Now past some enchanted isle
  In the moonlight sleeping fair,
We can almost see the while
  Elves and fairies dancing there;

On the breeze that wanders by

Notes of elfin music quiver,

And our boat goes silently

Floating, floating down the river.

MISCELLANEOUS POEMS.

KATIE BLOWING BUBBLES.

Katie, with thy laughing eyes
Full of sweet and glad surprise,
Gazing up towards the skies, —

Where thy bubble's rainbow hue
Floats between thee and the blue,
Listen, while I tell thee true.

Life has bubbles lighter far
Than your air-blown bubbles are,
Which one careless breath would mar!

Thou art yet too young to care

That thy face is very fair,

That so golden is thy hair;

And that yonder azure skies,

Where to-day no shadow lies,

Are not bluer than thine eyes!

Yes, thy greatest care to know

Where the earliest violets grow,

And wild honeysuckles blow;

Where the robin's young are nursed,

Where the wild grapes purple first,

And their burrs the chestnuts burst.

Katie, it were well for thee

If thy life might ever be

From all pride and envy free!

Trust not in thy beauty's power:
It is but a summer flower,
  Blooming, withering in an hour, —

As thy floating bubble there,
That a moment was so fair,
Burst, and vanished into air.

Seek thyself a surer dower, —
Knowledge, goodness, — these have power
Still to charm till life's last hour.

So when youth shall pass away,
And thy sunny locks are gray,
Thou canst wait a brighter day, —

Where no storms of time can blight;
Even Heaven's unfading light,
That shall never set in night.

LOOKING BACK.

" I would I were a child again!"

Too soon life's spring-time violets die;

Too briefly blooms the summer's rose,

Too soon morn's sapphire-tinted sky

With noontide's fiery splendor glows;

Too soon the greedy winds drink up

The dewdrop from the flower-cup;

Too soon the birds we tended fly;

And all too soon the heart grows old;

The thick warm blood creeps dull and cold,

And, looking back, we sigh with pain,

" I would I were a child again!"

"I would I were a child again!"

The shadow of the coming years

Across my pathway darkly lies:

My eyes àre not unused to tears;

Not passing drops from April skies,

But such as fall from eyes that see

Youth's fairy dreams and fancies flee

Without the power to bid them stay;

And gaze, and gaze like the charmèd bird,

With every pulse to madness stirred,

And stretch pale hands, and moan in vain,

"Oh, would I were a child again!"

Ah, were I but a child again,

To dream once more those happy dreams!

Reading from Nature's open books,

Learning of singing meadow-streams

And whispering pines and laughing brooks;

To feel, if but for one brief hour,

The same sweet consciousness of peace;

The strength to do, the will to dare,

That thrilled me in those early days

Ere I had tired of life's devious ways,

Or breathed the wild wish born of pain,

"I would I were a child again!"

THE POOR MAN.

Poor, yet rich indeed, am I :
   True, I rise at early dawning,
And my way to labor take
E'er the rich man is awake,
   Or while he, at most, lies yawning.

And the rich man looks on me
   With a scorn that needs no speaking;
Yet my heart is light as air,
While his brow is knit with care,
   And true pleasure shuns his seeking.

And I envy not the rich man,

    Though his rank in life is higher;

Better hands with labor reddened

Than a heart morose and deadened,

    Lost to every pure desire.

Can the rich more beauty find

    In the morning's sapphire splendor?

Do they taste a sweeter balm

In the noontide's breathless calm,

    Or the twilight soft and tender?

Does the gentle air of heaven

    Come more lovingly to woo them?

Sing the birds more loud or clear

When the rich man stops to hear,

    Than when I am listening to them?

He may boast his pictures olden

  Of Madonnas meek and sainted;

But I see in yonder blue

Pictures èvery hour new,

  By the heavenly Artist painted.

Mine are all the sweet wild flowers

  That the spring-time wakes to beauty;

Mine the forest zephyr-haunted;

Mine the songs by bright birds chanted,

  "Life is sweet, and joy a duty."

I have friends that truly love me,

  And I dearly, fondly prize them;

But the rich man never knows

Who are friends or who are foes,

  Till some freak of fortune tries them.

Men may fawn and cringe around him,

    Teaching servile tongues to flatter;

But when life's lamp burneth dim,

And death's angel calls for him,

    What will all his riches matter?

I shall sleep as sweetly then

    In some dim, unnoticed corner,

As if I had passed through life

Without care or toil or strife,

    Loaded down with wealth and pleasure.

A LEGEND.

Long time the weary knight had **rode in gloomy**
    silence on :
The stars were beaming in the sky, **the day's**
    last **beam was gone ;**
When, through the tangled wildwood deep, he
    sees a glimmering light,
And, faint and tired, his heart leaped up, and
    bounded with delight.

Now speed thee on, my **gallant** steed, and we
    will soon **be** there,
And better lodging shalt thou have than the
    dark forest lair ;

And soon, for all this **day's fatigue, thou shalt
  be well repaid**;
For nobly thou hast borne **me on across this**
  trackless glade.

And here I'll blow **my merry horn**, perchance
  that they may hear;
At least, 'twill while away the time, and **serve
  the** road to clear.
How dismally that raven croaks! 'tis ominous
  of ill,
Perchance 'tis but a **ghostly light; but** I will
  onward still.

Long time again **they wander** on : again at last
  they reach **the door.**
He knocks; no reply, — again, still louder than
  before.

But, though the voice of revelry resounds within

the wall,

No friendly hand unbolts the door ; none answered

to this call.

" Now, by my faith," the knight exclaims, " what

surly curs are here ?

Unbolt your door, good people all ! I would

partake your cheer."

No answer; knock again : " I ask if you refuse

the call..

By all the powers of heaven, I'll batter down

this wall !"

But, hark ! a rough and boisterous voice, " Seek

not to enter here ;

But shun it as ye fear to die : ye shall not taste

our cheer ;

And, if ye seek to enter in, this dog will take
away
The life you foolishly expose each moment of
your stay."

Then harshly on the night air still the dog's
wild howling broke,
And once again upon the air he heard the raven
croak;
And then again the house was still, all silent
as the tomb,
But still the cheerful light gleamed out upon
the forest gloom.

"Unbolt, unbolt!" again he cries, and once again
he knocks;
He hears the creaking of the bolt, the ringing
of the locks;

And once again that surly voice re-echoes through
    the gloom :
" Fool, thus to draw upon thyself a sure impend-
    ing doom ! "

And then the door is opened, and he enters
    boldly in,
And looks upon the glowing fire, the marble
    vase within.
But where are all the revellers? A lady young
    and fair
Is all the living thing his eyes can yet distin-
    guish there.

With courteous speech he bent his knee and
    sued for pardon there ;
And bright she smiled, but nothing spoke, that
    lady young and fair.

Then plentiful the board was spread with wines

    and costly cheer;

And, with this **token** of good-will, he had no

    thought of **fear.**

She **wore a wreath** upon her head, a wreath of

    roses bright;

She **plucked the fairest with her hand, so dainty**

    and so white;

And **then** she spoke: "I give you this. A token

    let it be,

What day it fades, **that** self-same day, **you'll**

    meet again **with me."**

She passed him, and she breathed "good-night;"

    and then she left the room,

And all was still and silent **as** the portals of

    the tomb;

And then upon the wall he saw a picture
  quaint and old:
'Twas sculptured by a master hand upon a
  shield of gold, —
A wounded, couchant deer it seemed within its
  forest lair;
But, oh! the eyes were human eyes: they glared
  upon him there,
And strangely seemed they to the knight to
  gaze where'er he moved.
Oh, dark and fatal was the spell: a potent spell
  they proved.

Day broke; the knight resumed his way; across
  his steed he throws
The bridle-rein, and in his belt he twines the
  blooming rose;

And, ere the sun the zenith gained, he reached
     his castle home,
And laughed and jested with his friends, and
     scorned the threatened doom.
A year had passed, still bloomed the rose; but
     on one fatal day
He found it pale and withering, and hasting to
     decay.
His heart within him loudly beat, his cheeks
     grew pale with dread,
And his eyes were dim and glassy as the eye-
     balls of the dead.

"I will not yield to this base dread, this weak,
     ignoble fear:
Ho, bring me forth my gallant steed! I go to
     chase the deer."

He mounted, waved a gay adieu, then, dashing
through the wood,
The clatter of the horse's hoofs awoke the solitude.
Soon from the road-side sprang a deer, a quick
and noble thing,
And joyously and free it moved as eagle on
the wing ;
And then an arrow keen he threw, and, wounded
in the side,
The noble animal turned back, red with life's
gushing tide.

Its graceful antlers pierced his steed, and, leap-
ing wild and high,
It gave one groan of agony, then laid it down
to die ;

And he, the knight, lay breathless there upon
the heathy plain,
And then the wounded deer returned, and stood
by him again;
Then, with a quick, impatient toss, it flung him
in the air;
And then, O God! those human eyes! they
gaze upon him there.
He knows them, and an icy chill shoots cold
through every vein:
His blood is flowing fast away; it stains the
sandy plain.

It turns away, it seeks the stream, it stems the
rippling tide:
He sees it clamber up the bank upon the farther side.

His life is ebbing fast away, and every heart-
    throb tells ;

But, rousing with a sudden start, he hears the
    chime of bells:

He sees the waters open wide ; he sees a woman
    rise :

'Tis she the lady of the wood, — he knows those
    mocking eyes.

She holds the faded wreath above, then lays it
    on his head ;

She keeps her vows, that wizard one: the knight
    is stiff and dead.

THE CARELESS GIRL.

There is a careless girl in school

Who often breaks each wholesome rule:

Her mind and manners both are rude ;

On others' rights she'll oft intrude.

Her looks bespeak a careless mind ;

Her tastes are few, yet unrefined ;

She nothing cares for others' peace,

Although it would her friends increase.

Her books are dirty, often torn ;

Her clothes are soiled before they're worn ;

And one might seek in vain to find
The slightest traces of a mind.

She may reform, be good and kind,
May cultivate her taste and mind,
Improve her manners and her fancy ;
And that she may, is the wish of Nancy.

THE CHILD AND ROSE.

A LOVELY child was roaming free
　Among the garden bowers,
And passed before a white-rose tree
　To gather of its flowers.

She twined a garland sweet and fresh;
　But, as she plucked a bud,
A sharp thorn pierced her tender flesh:
　The flower was stained with blood.

Thus, ever in the opening hours
　Of youth's bright sunny morn,
We grasp with eager haste life's flowers,
　And find, too late, the thorn.

TO SMOKERS.

There once was a day ere tobacco was
  known,
  Or snuff so extensively used,
When men were not found with cigar in their
  mouth,
  Or their noses so badly abused.

But snuff and tobacco are now all the rage;
  And a belle that was dressed for a ball
Without flowers in her hair would be rarer to
  find
  Than a man that would not smoke at all.

Then take my prescription, my beardless young

    friend :

Dash your pipe and cigar to the ground ;

Throw away your tobacco, — 'tis not fit to use, —

    And never a-smoking be found.

THE BRIDAL.

BRING bright orange-flowers from the south land,
    And twine in her gold-shadowed hair,
And gems from the depths of the ocean
    To flash on the white shoulders bare.
Our Lilly was born for a lady,
    And toil shall not harden her hand:
She shall mix in the gay halls of fashion
    With the high and the proud of the land.

Bring silk from the looms of the Indies,
    And plumes from the Paradise bird:
There ne'er was a face like our Lilly's;
    A voice like hers ne'er was heard.

Our Lilly, our own precious darling, —
　　And she is a rich man's bride, —
She shall ride in a soft, gilded carriage,
　　And nobles shall bow at her side.

There is a shade on her beautiful forehead,
　　Perchance of a transient pain:
Can it be that she looks on this splendor,
　　And sighs for her childhood again?
Does she think of the true heart that's bleeding,
　　She bartered for power and gold?
Does she dream of his talents and beauty
　　When she looks at the rich man old?

Oh, shame on our false-hearted Lilly,
　　That she should have stooped so low
To barter the peace of her childhood
　　For jewels and gilded woe!

For the love she has spurned and squandered
   She shall shed the bitterest tears,
And gold and gay splendor shall mock her
   In the life of her coming years.

THE FISHER.

Like an airy bubble the breath has blown,
  The fisher's boat lay on the water bright;
The sun looked down from his golden throne,
  And the waves leaped up with an answering
    light:
But the line flowed loose from his idle hand,
  And his eyes were turned to the glowing west;
For his heart was away in the distant land
  Where dwelt the friends that he loved the
    best.

When, oh! on his drowsy senses stole
  A strain of music, so soft and clear,

That it stirred the depths of the fisher's soul
  As he bent to the water his listening ear;
So sweet it flowed, that he scarce could tell
  From whence it came, while a strange emo-
    tion
Came soft as the sound of the vesper bell
  That trembles at eve o'er the placid ocean.

Then wilder and deeper numbers pealed,
  Sad as the sea in its troubled rest;
And he listened still to the magic notes
  With a strange, wild feeling within his breast.

WOMAN'S RIGHTS.

WHAT are the rights of woman? Is her place
Within the halls of loud and fierce debate?
Must she with men's stern energy keep pace,
To gain a name among the truly great?

Must she lead on to fields of mortal strife,
Or stand where muskets flash and cannon
roar?
Shall she forget the duties of her life,
To steep her hands in floods of human gore?

No: for her noblest mission is at home,
And never need she seek a different way,

Or in the path of stern ambition roam,

    While reason's star sheds its benignant ray.

'Tis hers to guide, to cherish, and direct

    The wayward steps of wild, impetuous youth;

'Tis hers to cheer, encourage, and protect

    The first unfolding germs of hope and truth.

Hers is a holy mission; for 'tis given

    To her to smooth life's rough, uncertain way;

To point the lone earth-wanderer up to heaven,

    Where all is perfect peace and endless day.

BORROWING TROUBLE.

Some people there are who find their chief

Enjoyment in real or fancied grief,

And they never seem to feel relief

  Till up to their eyes in trouble:

They delight in calling hope a cheat,

And pleasure poison because 'tis sweet,

And love a meteor bright but fleet,

  And friendship only a bubble.

If they take a journey to see a friend,

They are morally certain to apprehend

Their lives will come to a sudden end

  By some unforeseen disaster;

Or, if they venture to party or ball,

They are sure the ceiling or roof will fall,

And bury the company one and all

In the general devastation.

THE HOUR BEFORE EXECUTION.

DAYLIGHT at last! I thought the lagging hours
Of the long night would never wear away;
But, now that they are gone, my soul shrinks
    back,
Startlĕd, appalled, and trembles in itself
At its own nearness to eternity.

Daylight at last! Yon solitary star—
The only one that with a friendly beam
Invades my narrow dungeon—pales and fades
In morning's radiance; and the dim, faint light
That I have learned to watch for, and to call

My day, comes feebly struggling through the
    bars ;
And yet it must be sunrise. Ere an hour,
From the dark gallows, lifeless I shall swing,
While underneath the sea of human life
Surges and swells, and men with horrid jests
Mimic my agonies, and women crowd
To feast their eyes upon them. When this is
    o'er,
When my brief pangs are ended, and I hang
A blackened, lifeless weight, it will ebb back
This seething, surging wave of restless life
To mingle with the ocean-tides again,
Nor from its bosom miss the drop of spray.
Ah ! I could bear, methinks, the short-lived pain
Of dissolution, could I know that one
Of all this angry crowd that gather now
To clamor for my life, would shed a tear

Over my sufferings, or, with softened heart,

Think of me when I am gone; but well I know

No eye will brighten with a tear for me,

And in the years to come, when they recount

The story to their children, I shall be

Mentioned with loathing, and held up to them

As one who set at naught the laws

Of God and man, received at last the award

Of crime of murder. Oh, I little thought,

In childhood's days of innocence and peace,

To die a murderer on the gallows-tree!

God knows I had no murder in my heart:

I never meant to kill him. Hark! the hum

Of voices! Can the awful hour have come?

All night I heard the hammer's ringing sound,

And clink of plane and chisel as they smoothed

Boards for the narrow coffin that will be

My bed to-night; or, if my weary eyes

Closed for a moment, 'twas to dream I felt

The rope about my neck, and then I woke

With great, cold drops of anguish on my brow,

A sense of suffocation in my throat,

And mortal palsying of my limbs.

I thank thee, God of justice, that this blow

Descends on me alone: my gentle wife

Will never know the death her husband died.

My boy will never learn to hang his head

And glow with shame at mention of his sire;

For in my trial I have borne a name

That never was my own. Hark! 'tis the bell!

And in the passage I can hear the step

Of those who come to bear me to the place

Where I shall expiate my dreadful crime,

Giving my life for the life I took.

Farewell, my narrow dungeon! earth, farewell!

Father in heaven, hear my dying prayer!

Accept, I pray, my unfeigned penitence!

Go with me through the gloomy vale of death,

And grant, oh, grant to me the lowest seat

Within thy kingdom!

MAGDALENE.

THE night is dark and chill,

And the winds upon the hill

Moan like restless, troubled spirits, and are

never, never still.

The storm-king rides upon the blast, and shrieks

along the plain;

The mighty sea keeps sobbing with an almost

human pain;

And the dark and gloomy forest sighs a sor-

rowful .refrain.

To-night my thoughts go back,

O'er a withered, blasted track,

To the days of my lost happiness, that never
    can come back.
Oh! could they but return again, the sinless
    days of youth,
I would cleave unto their innocence and purity
    and.truth,
Closer than unto Naomi clung the loving-hearted
    Ruth.

    Oh, the dreary, dreary rain!
    How it beats against the pane,
And stands in dark and muddy pools along the
    narrow lane!
And in the churchyard far away, the church-
    yard old and new,
It drips with constant plashing sound upon a
    tall white stone,
And trickles down the narrow mound with long
    gray moss o'ergrown.

And the sleepers resting there,

Do they heed my dark despair?

Can they know my sin and sorrow, and not pity
even there?

In heaven, blessed mother, do you hear my
heart's deep cry?

Can you look with your pure vision on so vile
a thing as I,

Despairing, hating, loathing life, and yet afraid
to die?

If, from that sinless sphere,

You can see my wandering here,

If still you love the erring child, once so
dear,

Plead with the pitying Jesus that the precious
blood he spilt

May wash from my dark record all the damn-

    ing stain of guilt,

And admit me to those mansions for his ran-

    somed children built.

    I may not hope to gaze

    On the Saviour's glorious face,

Or stand before the great white throne, or tune

    my lyre to praise;

But, when the chain that binds me to this weary

    life is riven,

Haply that even unto me some blessing may

    be given,

And I may fill the lowest place in the bright

    court of heaven.

WAITING FOR A FRIEND AMONG BEASTS OF PREY.

Oh! saw ye e'er the startled dove
  Spread its white wings in graceful flight,
Then, circling in the blue above,
  Stoop earthward, and once more alight?
So fair, so graceful, and so wild
Is she, the Arab chieftain's child.
Eyes like twin stars upon a lake,
  Yet clear as some untroubled well,
And feet so light they hardly shake
  The fragrance from the lily-bell;
And, when around her father's home
  She like a ray of sunlight dances,

Her smiles light up his deepest gloom;
  He worships e'en her brightest glances.
It is the tranquil twilight hour:
  The fiery sun has gone to rest
  In his cloud-chambers of the west,
And she is sitting in her bower;
And at her feet a dark-eyed slave —
  One of a lovely captive band
Brought from a clime beyond the wave —
  Sings lays of her own father's land.
"Leave, leave me now," the maiden said,
"Bring thy companions to my bower."
With bounding step she leaves her side;
  And dancing girls, whose fairy feet
  Fall light as dew upon the flowers,
Round her in tinkling measures glide,
  And shake faint perfume round the bower;
But naught can charm the listless maid.

Her dark eyes fill with tears unshed,

And wearily her graceful head

Upon her downy couch is laid.

Three moons before, as gay she strayed

  Where she had often roved before,

Beneath the dark acacia shade,

  To tell her nurse orisons o'er,

  A lion, fiercest of its kind,

Upon her chosen lone retreat

Stole warily, with noiseless feet.

  And, as she homeward turned once more,

  She saw his shadow fall behind;

She saw him crouch with glaring eye,

And knew her time had come to die.

  Near, nearer yet the creature draws:

She cannot breathe, she cannot speak,

  She almost feels his savage claws

And hissing breath upon her cheek.

She shuts her eyes in wild despair;

She breathes one deep and heartfelt prayer,

"O Allah! save thy child."

She hears the sharp twang of a bow;

She hears the dreadful monster leap,

Then knows no more till she awakes

As from a long and troubled sleep;

And, bending over her, a form

That she had often seen in dreams,

With dark eyes in whose clear calm depth

A noble tender spirit beams;

And when a smile broke o'er his face

'Twas beautiful and strangely bright

As lightning in a stormy night.

Before her, at her very feet,

But cold and stiff, the lion lay:

It flashed upon her like a dream,

And shudderingly she turns away.

And now to-night she waits and prays

For him whom she has learned to love;

The moonlight o'er the waters plays;

The stars look brightly from above;

The beacon burns upon the tower;

Her father in his castle sleeps,

And she is waiting in her bower.

'Tis long beyond the appointed hour;

What wonder that she weeps.

"Alas, he will not come to-night,"

And wearily she turns away.

Hark! to the dipping of an oar!

She sees his frail boat near the shore,

And with a step as free and light

As the gazelle, whose silver feet

Scarce touch the earth they tread upon,

Down that dark, dizzy, winding height

She fearlessly has gone.

PLEASURE OF RAILROAD TRAVEL-LING.

Waiting in a dingy hovel
  On a cold November day,
Not one glimmering spark of fire;
  "Ticket-agent gone away."
Peering through the smoky windows,
  Opening wide the creaking door,
Prospect backward brakes and briers,
  Black and stagnant pool before.

Windows curtained well with cobwebs,
  Rafters smoky, bare, and black;

Old Boreas whistling rudely
    Through each widely gaping crack.
After two hours spent in waiting,
    You're inclined to bless your stars
When you hear the shrieking whistle
    And the rumbling of the cars.

Muttering with an inward chuckle, .
    "All is well that endeth well,"
You "propel" towards the door,
    Holding tight your "umberel."
Lo, "like streak of well-greased lightning,"
    Rushes past the iron steed :
Passengers all bow profoundly,
    Save a man that "wears a weed."

Just as you are grimly turning
    Fierce and desperate from the door,

You discover they are waiting

On a half a mile or more;

And the tall conductor mutters,

With an ominously black brow,

"Come, yer'd better be a startin';

Cars won't wait much longer nohow."

Leap at venture from the platform;

Never stop to find the stairs:

What if you should fall or stumble?

That is none of their affairs.

Brakeman tosses in your luggage,

Jams your bandbox all to smash;

You feel sure your trunk was breaking

When you heard that horrid crash.

Cars are filled to suffocation:

Vain are your imploring eyes;

No one offers to assist you,

   No one volunteers to rise.

And at length, worn out, perspiring,

   You are glad to take a pew

With a fat old Irishwoman,

   And her pail of onions too.

The effect is overwhelming;

   Soon the tears begin to flow:

Woman asks if 'tis her "onyins;"

   Says they don't affect her so.

Let me beg you keep your temper

   While you wipe your streaming eyes;

Think how worthy Job was tempted

   If your dander tries to rise.

Soon you reach the nearest station:

   Out the Irishwoman goes,

Bearing off aforesaid onions,
   Treading on your tenderest toes.
You may groan and sigh a little,
   And the tears may start anew:
No one minds it; all have business
   Without looking out for you.

Just as you are feeling better,
   Though your eyes are brilliant red,
Dandy, with a faultless dicky
   And a highly perfumed head,
Coolly takes the vacant corner;
   While you, blushing, shrink away
With (as if you didn't know it),
   "It is very cool to-day."

When, at length (if Heaven so wills it),
   You shall reach your destination,

Grumble not at cold and hunger ;

Thank your stars for preservation ;

Then a solemn declaration

Put on record with your pen,

To renounce steam locomotion

Evermore, Amen, Amen !

ONE HUNDRED YEARS AGO.[1]

I.

ONCE more with thankful hearts we greet
　　This glad returning day;
Once more within these walls we meet
　　To sing and praise and pray;
To offer grateful thanks to God
　　With hearts that overflow,
And trace the paths the fathers trod
　　A hundred years ago.

II.

A wild, unbroken solitude,
　　By foot of man untrod,

[1] Winchendon Centennial, 1864.

356

The grand primeval forest stood,

  And stretched green arms abroad ;

And where our church-bells call to prayer,

  And feet of hundreds go,

The wolf's long howl disturbed the air

  A hundred years ago.

III.

Our grandsires came with axe and plough :

  They felled the forest tree ;

Where fruitful fields are smiling now,

  They broke the stubborn lea ;

They laid foundations firm and broad ;

  They builded sure and slow :

We reap rich harvests where they sowed

  A hundred years ago.

IV.

They built them homes ; they tilled the

soil ;

Their flocks they watched and fed ;

With strong, brown hands inured to toil,

They won their daily bread ;

And, when the Revolution came,

They left the axe and plough,

And battled well in Freedom's name,

As we are battling now.

V.

Then honor to those men of old

Who felled the forest trees,

And warred with hunger, want, and cold,

That we might dwell at ease.

God give us strength our work to do,

   And grace our work to know,

Like those brave, simple men that lived

   A hundred years ago!

OLD AND NEW SCHOOLHOUSE.

FULL fifty years ago, in a schoolhouse small
and low,
With its long, hard, narrow benches standing in
a double row;
With its fireplace in the corner where the great
logs cracked and blazed,
And shot out fiery sparkles at which the children gazed;
And its tall desk in the centre, where they sat
who bore the rule,
Our fathers and our mothers — Heaven bless
them! — went to school.

All through the spring and summer days that
    glided slow away,
Our mothers learned to churn and spin ; our
    fathers turned the hay,
Or held the plough, or plied the hoe, or drove
    the team afield,
Or made the sturdy forest trees before their
    strokes to yield.
But when the winter came to end their long
    and busy toil,
When the biting winds blew fiercely, and the
    white snow wrapped the soil, —

To the old brick schoolhouse came they ; and
    still they love to tell
That 'twas there they learned to cipher and
    read and write and spell.

And there winter evenings, when the moon was
    full and bright,
And each small star shone and twinkled in the
    dusky brown of night,
They held their spelling-schools; and, when the
    spelling down was o'er,
Came the homeward walk by moonlight and
    lingering at the door.

Oh, the jokes and nods and blushes on the
    morrow when they met!
How bright eyes flashed with mischief, and red
    cheeks flushed rosier yet,
When was heard the busy whisper circling,
    spite of teacher's frown,
How "Jeremiah Tompkins went home with
    Sally Brown;"

Or how Ebenezer Parsons declares he saw a
light
In Deacon Jones's square room till the small
hours of the night!

Time flies away swiftly, and the works of man
grow old,
And at last the schoolhouse tottered, and walls
scarce stopped the cold;
Its benches creaked and tumbled, and its desk
bore many a trace
Of grotesque attempts at sculpture on its brown,
worm-eaten face:
So they reared another building, stronger, better than the last,
And the "old brick schoolhouse" grew to be a
memory of the past.

Meantime our village throve apace, and each suc-
ceeding year
Larger grew the troops of children who came
to study there;
And so our third new schoolhouse was built
upon the hill:
You may find some relics of it, if you go there,
standing still.
How great was our rejoicing! how large it
seemed and new!
But we kept on growing, growing, till we've
outgrown that one too.

We come to-night with willing feet, old age and
eager youth,
To dedicate this building to knowledge and to
truth;

To every eager learner shall its portals open free

In the sacred names of Justice and Right and
Liberty.

For those dear names the Pilgrims left their
homes across the sea

To seek some far-off country where their children might be free;

In those dear names our boys afar, on many a
Southern plain,

Bore the long and weary marches, and the hunger and the pain;

In those dear names they rallied round the
starry flag they bore;

In those dear names they conquered, and our
land is free once more.

There deigned of God to consecrate and bless
with power divine

This glad and free thankoffering at Learning's

sacred shrine.

Bless the teachers, bless the scholars, and, long

as it shall stand,

May it send forth men and women who shall

love and bless their land, —

Men and women pure in purpose, large of heart

and large of brain,

Who shall know the truth from error, and, so

knowing, dare maintain !

MY DREAM.[1]

As I sat by the window the other night,

Gazing out at the fading light,

And hearing the river's sullen roar

As it chafed and fretted its ice bound shore,

And watching the new moon's faint, mild beam,

I fell asleep, and dreamed a dream, —

A dream so wonderful, strange, and new,

That I couldn't help wishing it all were true.

I thought I was busy at work again,

And the hand of the clock had just reached

    ten,

[1] Spoken at school exhibition by O. A. Day.

When the door swung wide with a creaking
    sound;
And, turning quickly and sharply round,
I saw a stranger with eyes like flame,
And beard that down to his bosom came.

His flowing locks were white as snow;
And I thought, as he stood 'neath the lamp's
    bright glow,
That he only needed a scythe to look
Like "Father Time" in the picture-book.

He said, "You're sleepy and tired, I see:
Come! try your wings, and go with me."
"Wings!" cried I: "you are staring mad!
I haven't any, and never had."

But he smiled with such a knowing air,
That I looked at my shoulders again, and
    there,
Sure enough, grew a beautiful pair

That waved and fluttered like any bird's.

Now in dreams, you **know, the** most wonderful
change

Never strikes us as any thing strange;

And so, without wasting more time in words,

We rose from the earth as light as air,

And traversed the upper atmosphere.

We passed over city and crowded town,

Over wastes where only the stars looked down,

Over houses of virtue, and dens of crime

Where the fiery drink that turns the brain

Passed, with rude jests and oaths profane,

And the dice-box rattled, and cards were spread,

And men went in with a stealthy tread,

And the door was shut behind them fast.

I turned away with a shuddering dread,

For I knew that, when *next* that door they
passed,

Wealth, hope, virtue, and happiness, all
Would be gone beyond **the power of recall**.

Then over the boundless deep we flew
To lands where the skies are always blue;
Where **birds** always sing in the summer **bowers**,
And frosts never come to blight the flowers;
But the wail of the poor went ever up,
And misery mingled in poverty's cup.

Then I turned again to my own dear land,
Where toil and plenty go hand in hand,
And I tried **at last** to find my home;
But the strangest part is yet to come.

I thought I was wearied out at length,
And **my** wings seemed losing their airy strength,
And so we alighted upon a hill;
And **far** below us a village lay,
Through which a river wound **its way**,
That turned **the wheels of many a mill**.

Vine-wreathed cottages, neat and white,

Rose to my view in the soft moonlight;

And a neat white church, with its taper spire

That gleamed on my sight like an uplifted
hand

Pointing up to a better land.

"What a lovely scene!" I cried. He smiled

As he answered, "That is Bartonsville."

"That story's a falsehood," said I, "that's flat!

You can't expect me to swallow that:

Why, I came from there an hour ago."

He answered solemnly and slow,

"Over the earth ten years have passed

Since you beheld that village last."

"Oh, dear!" I cried: "what will people say?

They'll certainly think I have run away.

I wonder how long Moore's machine ran on

Before they found out that I was gone!"

Just then I heard somebody say,

"*Of all this world*, here's Osmond Day!

Wake up, wake up, and go to bed!

You'll certainly have a cold in your head."

I opened my eyes with a sudden start,

And saw my mother's jolly face

Looking the picture of wild amaze,

With eyes wide open, and lips apart.

So I took the candle, and said "good-night;"

But my dream still haunted my wakeful brain,

And I turned it over again and again.

'Twas a dream so wonderful, strange, and new,

That I couldn't help wishing it all were true;

And now you've heard it, my friends, don't you?

INVOCATION TO SLEEP.

Come to my pillow, sweet angel of sleep!

Over my forehead thy magic wand sweep;

Close the pained eyes that are longing for rest;

Fold my tired form to thy shadowy breast;

Clasp in thy cool palm my feverish hand;

Lead me away to thy own fairyland;

Let me forget to repine or to weep:

Come to my pillow, sweet angel of sleep!

Come, and bring with thee a store of bright
    dreams;

Let me wander again by my own mountain
    streams;

Let me gather spring violets down in the dell,

And drink once again from the mossy old well;

Let me hear the glad song of the robin that

     made

Her nest every year in the apple-tree's shade;

Over my soul let the olden peace creep:

Come to me, beautiful angel of sleep!

Come, for the night dew is closing the flowers

To sleep, with shut petals till morn's rosy

     hours;

Birds lightly rock in their leaf-curtained nest;

Daylight's last crimson fades out from the

     west;

And, as I gaze at the fathomless sky,

Bright Hesper glitters through tears in my eye.

Why should I waken to sorrow, and weep?

Come at my bidding, O angel of sleep!

All the day long have I mixed with the crowd,

Noisy and heartless, and jostling and loud.

"Each for himself" seemed their motto to be:

Why should they care for a stranger like me?

Now from the tumult and strife I have fled,

Seeking but vainly repose for my head:

Come, and my soul in forgetfulness steep,

Come to me, come to me, angel of sleep!

BERTHA'S CHRISTMAS.

Bertha was out in the frosty street,
  And the night was fierce and wild;
The ice-work wounded her small bare feet,
  For she was a beggar-child;
The snow fell faster and faster still,
  As blindly she wandered on,
Till it seemed that her very heart was chill,
  And her power to move was gone.

She sees the lamps of the city glow
  Like stars from the azure cast;
The sweet bells chime out o'er the crispy snow,
  And music is borne on the blast:

There is joy, there is plenty, but not for her ;

And the tears rain down apace,

And freeze into glittering diamond beads

On the pallid and want-pinched face.

All day she has wandered : the chillness and snow

Have fallen on her aching head ;

But her weary limbs can no farther go :

She sinks in her freezing bed.

Oh, joy ! she is weary and faint no more :

It is gone, — that tremor and pain ;

And her feet, that erst were so cold and sore,

They are growing warm again.

Drowsily shuts she her dark-blue eye,

Dimmed by the want and pain ;

Then to the dome of the midnight sky

Turns she her gaze again.

She saw mid the broken clouds a star;
    And, while she looked and smiled,
It changed to the face of her dead mamma,
    And beamed on the beggar-child.

She comes still nearer, and now she stands
    By the happy Bertha's side;
She raises her up with gentle hands
    As she did before she died;
Then steadily, slowly, they upward rise
    Above the cold, pitiless storm:
There is light and love in the upper skies,
    And the beggar-child is warm.

They found her there in the icy street,
    All pallid and stark and cold;
But in her face was a smile so sweet,
    That they paused again to behold.

A narrow box and an unmarked grave
  To the body frail was given;
But a place in the loving Father's arms
  Was Bertha's for aye in heaven.

O ye who know not of cold or storm,
  Of hunger or want or care,
When ye come to pass to the spirit-land,
  Shall ye better than Bertha fare?
Will He pause to think of your pride or power?
  Can you bribe Him with glittering gold?
Will He list to your prayers in that awful hour
  When the secrets of hearts are told?

If unto His weary and wandering ones
  You succor and peace have given,
How sweet on your ear will fall their tones
  As they welcome you up to heaven!

But, if ye have slighted their tears and sighs,

How stern will the verdict be!—

"Inasmuch as ye gave no meat to these,

Ye have given it not to Me."

THE OUTCAST.

She stood outcast from human love,
  In solitude and woe;
Her childhood's peace, that heavenly dove,
  Had left her long ago;
The murky clouds hung thick above,
  And the river rolled below.

Its waves were swift and dark and deep:
  She listened to their roar;
She watched the current's onward sweep,
  Drifting dead weeds ashore,
And wished she was but safe asleep
  In her father's house once more.

They are safely housed from the pelting storm,
   My brothers and sisters all;
The very chief one asleep and warm,
   And Carlo lies in the hall;
While the raindrops fall on my shrinking form,
   And drop from my tattered shawl.

Then she listened again to the tempest's wail,
   And looked at the frowning sky,
And shook with fear as the fitful gale
   Went moaning and shrieking by;
And her cheeks grew still more deathly pale,
   And wilder her tear-dimmed eye.

She thought of her early sinless hours,
   Ere sorrow or pain she knew,
When she bounded away from the garden bowers,
   When her bare feet felt the dew;

And fair and sweet as her own bright flowers,
She daily and hourly grew.

She knelt with her thin hands raised on high:
"O Father in heaven!" she cried,
"Look down from thy throne in the azure sky
For the sake of Him who died,
And forgive my sins of darkest dye
For the love of the Crucified!"

A pause, a plunge, and the water cold
Has closed o'er the sinking head;
And the deep, black waves, like a shroud, en-
fold
The form of the early dead;
And the waves and the festering mould
Are the weary one's last bed.

O pious souls who her sins condemn,
Who fast and pray so much,
Who joy that in Jesus' diadem
There will be no room for such, ·
No more shall your saintly garment's hem
Be polluted by her touch!

And when in His temple you are found,
O chosen worshippers!
Draw closely the heavy mantle round,
And arrange the costly furs;
Then thank your God with a joy profound
That your sin is not as hers!

THE OLD AND THE NEW YEAR.

Through frosted panes the moon's cold light
    Gleams faintly round the chamber dim;
The Year is dying with the night,
    And you and I will watch with him.

The good Old Year! We owe him much:
    He brought us joy, unknown till then;
He strewed our path with pleasures, such
    As life can never give again.

And if he sometimes led our feet
    Through narrow pathways thorn-beset,

And if sometimes Hope's blossoms sweet
  With Disappointment's tears were wet, —

If some of youth's fair dreams are fled,
  Enough are left to gild the way;
For every tear he made us shed
  He gave as many a happy day.

New friends he gave us, who are dear;
  He spared the old ones dearer yet:
We cannot choose but drop a tear,
  And close his eyes with deep regret.

Into the future dim we peer,
  And question with a doubting heart,
What hast thou brought for us, New Year?
  Shall we with thee as kindly part?

The clock peals out the midnight hour :
  It is the Old Year's funeral knell,
And its next chime with thrilling power
  Will of a New Year's advent tell.

Father, to all thy universe,
  Of every tongue and every creed,
May this fair day just dawned on us
  Become a "glad New Year" indeed !

And wheresoever on earth's wide plain
  A single suffering soul may dwell, —
To the poor Ethiop in his chain,
  Or the sad prisoner in his cell ;

To all thy creatures bending low
  Beneath Oppression's heavy sway,

May this New Year, begun in woe,

End in a gleam of brighter day!—

The day when men of every blood

Before Thy glorious throne shall fall,

Owning our common brotherhood,

And one great Father of us all!

THE DEATH OF KANE.

Far o'er the ocean comes a dirge
  For one in manhood's prime laid low,
And with the murmur of the surge
  Is blent a deeper note of woe;
And eyes to-day with tears are dim
  That never saw for whom they weep,
And hearts are bowed with grief for him
  Who sleeps the long and dreamless sleep!

All vain love's agonizing care
  To charm away the pangs of pain!
All vain the balmy southern air
  To bring back life and health again!

The dauntless nerve, the iron will,
  The cheek that danger never paled,
Strong arm and noble heart are still
  In death's dark night forever veiled.

The eyes that watched the long, long night
  Beneath the pole-star's icy ray,
And hailed the first faint tinge of light,
  Precursor of the longed-for day,
Are closed on earth forevermore;
  And dull for aye the ears will be
That erst have heard the sullen roar
  And ice-breaks of the northern sea!

Yet, while we feel the chastening rod,
  And 'neath the heavy burden lie,
Still let us thank a gracious God
  That brought the loved one home to die.

Thank God! O bleeding hearts bereft,
  And crushed beneath the heavy blow,
Your loved one's relics were not left
  To bleach amid eternal snow.

And if life be not length of days,
  But worthy deeds and well-earned fame,
How few have lived to earn the praise
  That clusters round thine honored name!
The dauntless leader gone before,
  His bright example left to bless:
Heaven has one shining angel more,
  And earth, one noble son the less.